SIMEON
CROOM
and the
TREASURE STAR

THE CHRONICLES OF CROOM, BOOK I
STEVEN LUNA

Dapper Press, LLC
Phoenix · Chicago

The characters and events portrayed in this book are fictitious. Any similarity to real persons, living or dead, is coincidental and not intended by the author.

ISBN 978-0-9965121-7-6

FREE BOOKS, YOU SAY?
OH YES, I SAY...

Join my reader's group, and you can have any book I've ever written absolutely free. Plus, you'll find out about all the good stuff I've got coming up before anyone else. You can't lose.

Visit www.thestevenluna.com and sign up!

OTHER BOOKS BY STEVEN LUNA

Joe Vampire
Joe Vampire: The Afterlife
Joe Vampire: The New Paranormal
Songs from the Phenomenal Nothing
Starfire and the Miracle Tree
This is Why We Can't Have Nice Things

For Vince Carbajal,
who once said I might want to think
about publishing my books myself.
I wouldn't have started this whole shebang
without your encouragement.
Thank you for that.

ONE

Haven City, 1936

To say that Simeon Croom was a man of extraordinary talents would be like saying the sky is wide, or babies are noisy, or the pope has a fondness for tall hats—an understatement the likes of which can only be illustrated by poor comparisons using ridiculous imagery. Anyone who made his acquaintance for longer than twelve seconds would have known that he was capable of playing violin concertos blindfolded, and with the bow held between his toes; that he could recite sonnets and soliloquies while balancing a dagger on the tip of his tongue; that he could speak seventeen languages, including one that required a mouthful of marbles, and another he'd invented himself simply because the others lacked adjectives that effectively expressed his own self-professed magnificence (he called it Simeonese), though French was not among them. They would have learned all of this about him before they'd even finished shaking his hand.

Because Simeon Croom would have told them so himself.

The man loved few things as much as he loved making a big first impression.

Key among Croom's prodigious talents was a little-known skill called sanguinial meditation, a practice which allowed him to conduct the elements in his bloodstream by willful control of his autonomic nervous system. He'd stumbled upon it during a cultural studies assignment while rooting through the writings of Cyril Mallowicke, a sociologist who discovered the phenomenon occurring among the people of the Jakotu rainforest. It worked like this: whenever a member of the tribe was licked by a deadly blathertoad or stung by a lethal needlebeak beetle (both of which happened with miserable frequency), the victim would simply sit upright against a tree with a coconut on his head and enact the meditation to separate toxin from blood and route it harmlessly to the appendix, thereby preventing absorption into the vital organs and sparing his own life. It was nothing short of a physiological miracle, though the significance of the coconut was something of a mystery. When Croom made the discovery during his freshman year at Mount Tumbledown University, he practiced every day until he became a master, coconut and all. He may never have encountered a blathertoad or a needlebeak beetle on campus, but when it came to over-imbibing with the entire charter of the Sigma Sigma fraternity, Croom was able to use sanguinial meditation to route the alcohol in his blood to his appendix and remain stone-cold sober no matter how much liquor he consumed. This trick allowed him to drink anyone he encountered under the table, and over the table, and back under it again, as many times as he pleased. And though his college days were long past, Croom was still in possession of this curious and purposeful ability. Unfortunately for him, in order to initiate it, he had to be fully sober.

And at the moment, he was anything but.

He also had no coconut.

The crowd at Murphy's Pub made a shameless circle around him as he performed like an escaped circus monkey who'd picked the lock on his cage with his own tail. The ungodly amount of alcohol coursing through him had inspired front flips from the tabletops and cartwheels along the bar, spurred on by a chorus of chants and hoots from the onlookers. There had even been a few imitators joining in on the antics, lily-livered copycats who'd tried their best but simply couldn't keep up and were now lying in various awkward positions against the bar after losing consciousness. For even without sanguinial meditation to cleanse his bloodstream, Croom was still the heartiest drinker in any bar he entered, and he always became far more entertaining when under the influence.

"I could do this all night, you know," he said as he spun past. "And not be the least bit dizzy when I'm finished."

Murphy's also happened to be graced by the presence of its second-heartiest drinker: Croom's colleague, oldest friend, and most enthusiastic competitor from college, Horatio Bombfell. He was the only man in the bar who'd been able to match Croom's exuberant antics. "Then you should have worn your pajamas and brought your toothbrush," he replied. "Because *I* could do this all night, too."

Bombfell was a braggart in his own right, an overachiever whose list of stellar accomplishments rivaled Croom's litany of grand talents. According to himself, Bombfell had scaled the highest peak of the Migoola Range in the Upper Sephrades in search of famed mountain climber Lance Heraldstaff, just to return a canteen he'd borrowed during a previous camping trip; he'd traveled into regions uncharted and planted flags with his emblem on them (a black circle containing a falling bomb emblazoned with a B, for reasons both obvious and unimaginative) to stake his claim, though sometimes those lands were already fully populated and in no need of being claimed at all. He'd even had a small island off the coast of Phenocia named for him by the elder of the clan who lived there, though the Great Noble Empire had an entirely different idea about what to call it, considering that the territory actually belonged to them.

But his bold statements about equaling Croom's shenanigans could not be refuted, especially not by those who were watching as it happened.

"Then I guess we'll be greeting the sunrise together!" Croom said as he turned three nimble handsprings, then threw in a pike and a double-aerial, just to show off.

"It wouldn't be the first time, would it?" Bombfell countered as he spun in a layout with a triple full-twist at the end. He wasn't one to be outdone. "We'll just keep going, well into tomorrow if necessary!"

Murphy himself, however, had something entirely different to say about things. "Listen up, you two: you're makin' a royal mess of my bar—*again*. There's broken chairs all over the place, and the tables have overturned and gone all wobbly...not to mention the drunk guys litterin' the place tryin' to outdo y'both. And which of you will be payin' for all the bottles you've blown through? That bourbon you love don't come cheap."

There was a pile of cash on the table, mostly dollar bills that were soft and damp and terribly wrinkled, laid out by the onlookers as the stakes climbed ever higher. "Not to worry, Murph," Croom assured him, hardly even out of breath despite his frenzied gymnastic display. "The tidy sum on the table will be yours to cover the tab for the whole bar and any damages we've caused when this numb-skull finally surrenders and I win it all."

"What my delusional friend here means, Mr. Murphy," Bombfell corrected, "is that *I'll* gladly cover the cost of cleaning up your charming establishment once he drops from exhaustion and the winnings come to me."

Murphy grunted, a sound that seemed to come from the bottom of his phenomenally substantial belly. "Then y'won't mind if I just take my pile and settle it all up now, thank you very much." He said it loudly and deliberately as he gathered the bills and stuffed them into his apron, but the somersault competition had begun, and the two men hardly even noticed.

It was sometime near three-thirty a.m.—well after closing time, but before the competition shifted from acrobatics to judo—when Croom realized there was nothing at stake for him anymore, or for Bombfell, for that matter. "Murphy took the money hours ago…everyone sobered up and left shortly afterward," he said on ragged breath, finally winded from the ridiculous non-stop activity.

Bombfell had his feet curled around his ears and was rounding the bar on his belly like a wagon wheel in a strange display of flexibility and perpetual motion. "So he did…so he did."

"What say we finish up with a quadruple back-flip?" Croom suggested. "Whoever lands the final flip first is the victor."

Bombfell hesitated. Whether it was due to consideration of Croom's suggestion or his own encroaching exhaustion in spite of his protest to the contrary, only he knew for certain. "We could definitely do that, old friend, if you think it advisable."

"I believe I do, Horatio," Croom said.

"Then we shall," Bombfell agreed.

The two men sprang to their feet and squatted low in equally defensive stances. "On my three," Bombfell proclaimed. "One...two..." He was in the air before he even reached three, which was very much how he engaged every competition: giving himself an unfair advantage whenever possible.

Fortunately for Croom, he knew his dear friend was prone to such deceit.

He was in the air on Bombfell's two as well.

Both men performed their quadruple backflips admirably...though rather than either landing the last one on their feet as intended, both men landed flat on their backsides—Croom at the far side of the room against the wall, Bombfell in a corner of the bar that Murphy failed to sweep on a regular basis, if the pile of cocktail stirs and discarded gum was any indication.

"A draw, then," Croom declared as he slowly crawled back to the table.

"It does appear that way," Bombfell agreed as he crept toward center ground as well.

"Smashing," Croom huffed, finally exhausted as he sank into his chair. "For the record, though...it was you who decided to quit."

Bombfell pressed heavily on the table as he plopped into the chair opposite Croom. "But *you* were the one who suggested it, Simeon."

"But *you* could have declined the offer, Horatio."

They were even competitive about ending their competitions.

"A draw on the draw, then," Bombfell said authoritatively, for all the good he knew it would do.

Croom refused to make the concession himself. "If you say so!" he said cheerfully.

Bombfell finally relented as he stretched his legs out

before him and straightened himself into relative comfort. "Well...that was one of our longer contests, if not one of the more rewarding."

"Yes," Croom agreed, flexing the circulation back into his hands. His knuckles cracked like peanut shells. "Is it possible we're getting too old for this nonsense?"

"Speak for yourself!" Bombfell jibed. A quarter-bottle of Phineas Goodsense's Proprietary 40-Proof Oak-Cured Bourbon that remained on the table split nicely in two as Bombfell filled their glasses for one final round. "I hardly felt a thing the whole time."

Croom scoffed. "Bah! You were three jump-kicks away from your heart exploding, if the ruddy flush in your forehead has anything to say about it."

Bombfell pounded his meaty fist on the table. "Blowhard!"

Croom pounded his in return. "Bigmouth!"

The men glared at one another as the sheer folly of their display dawned on them. Then their stern faces broke like party balloons, and they laughed deep and manic laughter that would have pegged them as certifiably insane under any other circumstances—and perhaps even under *these* circumstances, had anyone been around to hear it.

"Age is for whiskey and cheese!" Bombfell declared.

"For mummies and wine!" Croom proclaimed.

"For relics and temples and ruins!" Bombfell threw in.

"And we are timeless—infinite and eternal, no matter how our heads might silver or our faces might crease!" Croom decided with his glass raised, and Bombfell raised his as well. "Hear! Hear!" they cried together. It was the first time they'd agreed on anything all night.

Possibly in the previous decade.

Bombfell stared wistfully into the amber nectar in his glass. "Tell me, Simeon: do you remember our trip to Naboor to locate the Golden Claw?"

Croom blinked determinedly, which was a language all its own. "If you mean do I remember flying in a sky-blue barnstormer missing half of its wing bolts and losing its propeller as we dropped ten thousand feet over the course of two minutes and made a parachute landing in the desert, only to be captured by the armed guard of King Mahali who believed us to be assassins for the Royal Military Guard even though we had no weapons—which was incredibly foolish of us, considering we were on a hunt for ancient treasure that belonged to a culture known for executing infidels by feeding them to giant spider-crabs—and no credentials that explained who we actually were, and only after we accepted his challenge to learn and recite the Naboor national anthem by heart, even though neither of us had bothered to learn Naboori, but I picked it up in minutes because I'm just that adept at language acquisition, and lucky for us that I am because it saved our bacon long enough for us to drop sleeping serum in everyone's chalices so we could break into the treasure room, only to learn that the so-called Golden Claw was being used as a doorstop, just before the bodyguards awoke and alerted the palace sentries that two rakish thieves with spectacular smiles and magnificent hair had drugged the king and were now fleeing the palace, after which they launched a barrage of arrows and spears in our direction as we fled for our lives and stole away on a steamer dressed as peasant women, sailing for two weeks back across the sea until we were home again and the Golden Claw safely in the hands of the Hydewhite Museum for the Preservation of Uncommon Artifacts, where it would be treated with the dignity and respect afforded only the most sacred of ancient treasures...then yes. I remember that." Then Croom smirked, which was one of his more endearing expressions, second only to his furrowed brow of smug yet reluctant confusion. "Vaguely."

"You scoundrel!" Bombfell barked. "You remember it as well as I do!"

Croom's gaze went starry. "It was one of our more rousing encounters with royalty, I'd say."

"Perhaps the grandest of all our adventures! And certainly you remember being chased by the headhunters of Kravak Village a year later, with you driving that three-tired jalopy after we scavenged their cobalt funerary urn?"

"Scavenged?" Croom grimaced. "I prefer 'recovered for preservation purposes.'"

Bombfell crowed. "And the time we rode roughshod on donkeys down into the bowels of the Greater Boraleus Canyon and discovered the fabled Vibranium Crystal Caverns and plucked a collection of their points for further study, only to realize they were all interlinked, and that we'd set off a minor intercavern avalanche?"

Croom smiled fondly at the memory. "I coined the term 'cavernlanche' on that trip."

"And remember when we—"

"Yes, yes," Croom interrupted as he drained his glass in one great swig, "we've had our fair share of swashbuckling and derring-do, Horatio...not to mention the tips of our mustaches sliced off by unexpected swordplay and arrows shot toward our arses more times than either of us should care to mention. And I know *you* as well as I know the annals of our travelogue...I hardly believe you've shown up in Haven City out of the blue just to get sauced on Goodsense and have a cartwheel contest with me before chatting about old times. That doesn't feel genuine."

"A fellow can't come home to reminisce with his dear friend over drinks without having other motives?" Bombfell asked. "Isn't the rekindling of a long-held friendship reason enough to return?"

Bombfell's face did a fair impersonation of innocence, though it wasn't enough to fool Croom. "Not when the fellow in question is you."

Bombfell winked, which was never a good sign, and hardly as charming as it was meant to be. "You've always been rapier-sharp, even when loaded to the gills on expensive liquor."

Croom took the compliment, but wouldn't be dissuaded by it. "Actually, the somersaults seem to have brought renewed clarity. Now tell me why you're here—something that bears a closer resemblance to the truth this time."

It had taken nine bottles of Goodsense and seven hours of competitive physical exertion that ultimately led to a tie, but Horatio Bombfell finally got down to brass tacks. "I've been wondering of late, with all of the globetrotting we've done in search of such grand and mysterious artifacts, if perhaps we might have missed a thing or two."

Croom's forehead rumpled like an old man's sweater. "I'm certain we've missed *many* a thing or two. But we've left that sort of traipsing about for the next generation of discoverers. The mantle has been handed over, and we're both onto the next phases of our lives—me curating and lecturing at the museum, and you doing...tell me again what it is that you've been doing with your time since we last spoke?" Of all the things Croom remembered, the present seemed to evade him almost entirely.

Bombfell's expression turned as sincere as possible, which meant it still aroused a fair amount of suspicion, though far less than it had in times past. "I've been pining, Simeon."

"Pining?"

"Yes, pining—for the past; for our adventures together. For new discoveries and unseen vistas and long-forgotten trinkets that lie deep in their crypts, whispering our names whilst waiting for us to unearth them, wondering if we'll ever arrive…"

Croom laughed again. "Your flair for the dramatic hasn't diminished in the least."

"I wouldn't be me without it." Bombfell waited for Croom's excitement to kick in, but it did no such thing. "Can you honestly tell me you haven't wondered what it would be like to have one last barrel roll through the wild blue yonder and run in serpentine as we elude primitives hurling fiery bolas at our heads while cradling some wondrous delight believed to be nothing but a figment of ancient imaginations, but in which we had faith enough to seek out, to go forth and make the discovery? Something we found by sheer ingenuity and canny wit and refusal to surrender in the face of insurmountable odds?"

"Do these odds come with a king-sized mattress and a frosted pint of lager resting on the nightstand?" Croom asked. "Because if they don't, then I'd have to say…"

His answer faltered before he could finish.

Bombfell saw it finally: the familiar, dreamy haze of imagined adventure cast over his friend's boyish face. "Aha! You *do* miss it!"

It couldn't be denied. "Of *course* I miss it," Croom confirmed. "But I've found comfort in familiarity, in stability…and in not having a near-decapitation be the highlight of my day."

"You say 'near-decapitation' as if it's a bad thing," Bombfell chided.

In all honesty, Croom *had* daydreamed quite frequently about how much more there was left to discover; he was faced with it every day, in fact, in a museum that had more empty space than it had fascinating exhibits. There was always room for something new, and always something new awaiting discovery.

"What would we even be in search of at this point?" Croom asked. "Not that I'm necessarily interested, mind you...it would have to be something incredibly worthwhile for me to give up my nightly post-museum relaxation time." He heard himself, and was slightly horrified at how settled he sounded, how lacking in intrepid spirit.

Bombfell heard the exact same thing, and his eyes shone with promise and opportunity at the sound of it. "Well...we could start with the Knotted Staff of Piltoch. It was one we always intended to—"

Croom shook his head. "Dunville Weatherton unearthed it five years ago...I thought for sure you'd heard."

"Oh. That's unfortunate. I guess I haven't kept up as well as I thought." Bombfell wouldn't be deterred. "Then we can go after Hesperod's Jade. There's bound to be a passage into the trove just—"

"That was found as well, claimed by Ulysses Frock for the Duke of Hillsburg about six months ago."

"Frock? That rapscallion."

"The word I used when I heard wasn't quite so complimentary," Croom sighed. His discoverer's envy was in full swing now.

"Dash it!" Bombfell cried. "It seems I haven't kept up at all." His fingertips drummed rapidly against one another as his thoughts wandered through a wish list of things left to be sought. "I suppose there's always the Treasure Star of the Zingaloo…"

"Now *that* one…I know nothing of." It wasn't like Croom to be lacking knowledge about a lost treasure or a fabled relic. He felt a pang of inadequacy, though it was such a foreign and unprecedented feeling, he didn't recognize it at all and summarily dismissed it as gas.

Bombfell grinned. "No?"

"No. I can't say that I've even heard the name before."

Bombfell sighed with great relief. "Safe to say this sweet treat is still on the list, then," he said, and his happy grin spread into a smile that shone like a sharp crescent moon in a clear night sky.

And it had nothing to do with Goodsense.

TWO

"Over two thousand years ago," Bombfell began, his voice dropping an octave or so until it settled into his most theatrical storyteller range, "deep in the rumbling green heart of the Sarabezi jungle, there lived a tribe of gatherer-mystics called the Zingaloo, whose lives were guided by the belief that the stars were actually gods. They had three-and-a-half times the number of constellations as any other recorded culture in history, and their mythology included stories of shamans who could locate the most significant of stars, even in the full light of day."

Croom was hardly impressed by this. "*Everyone* can locate the most significant of stars in the full light of day," he scoffed. "It's called the sun."

"Ah, but this star wasn't the sun...it was another that shone below the sun, like a little brother. It was called the Treasure Star, or as it was pronounced in their language, *thoiink-thwip.*" It was more of a sound effect than a word.

Croom's face crinkled like a paper bag. "Do you have a hair on your tongue, Horatio?"

"This was their language, Simeon," Bombfell explained. "They spoke in pops and whistles and tongue thwips and water doinks."

"And what is a water doink, exactly?" Croom asked.

"This." Bombfell flicked his cheek with his middle finger and pushed air out of his mouth as if he were trying to spit, which resulted in the sound of a stone dropping into water.

"Ah!" Croom said, charmed by the silliness of the whole spectacle. "And you know this how?"

"Because my esteemed colleague Dr. Eddington Twill was an expert in both the Sarabezi region and the long-extinct Zingaloo people. He spent the majority of his professional life learning their stories, deciphering their pictograms, and bringing their long-extinct language to life. He postulated that their linguistic building blocks arose from their trying to spit out bugs and feathers, and somehow it all turned into Zingali."

"Was he sober the entire time he did this?"

"No," Bombfell said seriously. "He wasn't."

If there was one thing Simeon Croom loved more than a good adventure or an ancient relic awaiting recovery, it was a mysterious primitive culture whose language had been interpreted with the aid of liquor. He had his listening ears on now. "And what was it that made this little star so significant?"

"It was said to be set in the sky by one of their own in an effort to save the tribe from the wrath of their gods."

"Oh....well," Croom said. "I suppose that is pretty significant."

Bombfell sighed. "One of their primary myths told of a revered Zingaloo shaman named Ubwoop who sought to commune with the gods in hopes of absolute transcendence. He traveled deep into the heart of the jungle when the moon was new, the sky was dark, and the stars shone their brightest. He laid on his back in a posture of total surrender and watched the skies intently as he practiced the Zingaloo ritual of *Bagwhiiiip-whiiip-whiiip*, which translates to 'The Great Heavenly Hellos.' He focused on one star-god at a time, gazing fervidly at it and speaking its name, inviting it to reveal its wisdom, then moving onto the next one, until he'd greeted every single star-god in the pantheon. This would be the equivalent of saying 'Gooday!' to every citizen in Haven City seventeen times over, all in the same night."

"Gracious!" Croom exclaimed. "I don't even say hello to them once a *year*—not even at the Forayngle Park summer picnic."

"Such was the depth of Ubwoop's faith in his gods," Bombfell said. "When he was finished, he was greeted by a column of green fire that carried the gods down into the jungle, led by a figure the Zingaloo called Shtaaa." The sound came from the back of Bombfell's throat, as if he were relieving it of an itch.

Croom's eyebrows rose like a drapery. "Well, that one doesn't sound like spitting out bugs, does it? It sounds more like the empty space between stations on a radio dial."

"May I continue?" Bombfell said, his irritation clearly visible. "I haven't gotten to the good part yet."

"By all means, Horatio—press on!"

Bombfell smiled begrudgingly. "Thank you. To show their gratitude for his devotion, the gods bestowed upon him a jeweled orb that represented the very treasure of the universe: life itself. The orb was a source of great power, you see, said to extend indefinitely the lives of all who lived in its presence. It was the transcendence he'd been seeking, the gift of immortality, and Ubwoop was overwhelmed to receive it. The only expectation was that it be shared with the other Zingaloo—the gods were very clear on this; there would be grave consequences if their request weren't heeded. Then Shtaaa and the other gods rode their column of fire back to the heavens, and the shaman was left with the orb, and the very best intentions of returning to the village to share his gift with the whole tribe. But as he held the orb, he very quickly fell under a shadow of selfishness and greed that belied his better nature. The gods were rewarding *him* for his devotion, he decided; the rest of the tribe had done nothing to curry favor with them, and therefore they deserved none. So rather than returning to the Zingaloo village, Ubwoop retreated further into the depths of the jungle with his orb to live out his eternal years alone."

"That irrepressible imp!" Croom squawked.

"Indeed. When he didn't return, his family searched for him, but he hid from them every time, so that all they found was his mad laughter resounding through the trees. Eventually, he came to be regarded as a type of jungle specter the Zingaloo called a *wooosk-whikwhik*—a spirit that had gotten lost on its way to the next world."

"That's lovely, isn't it?" Croom said. "In its own unusual way."

Bombfell ignored his friend's interjection. "Two hundred years after Ubwoop abandoned the tribe, a young Zingaloo boy named Thoiink was out in a deep jungle thicket gathering bulbs and berries for his family's supper, which just happened to be the very spot where Ubwoop had received the orb centuries earlier, when a column of green fire broke through the canopy, and Shtaaa and the other star-gods appeared before him as they had appeared to the shaman. Thoiink fell to his knees in terror as they asked for their orb back. The young Zingaloo told them the story as he knew it: that the old man they'd given the orb had kept it for himself, that he'd never returned from the jungle and was nothing more than a ghost now. It wasn't the answer they were expecting."

"I would think not," Croom agreed.

"The gods were so angered that their generosity had come to such a selfish end, they caused the earth beneath Thoiink's feet to rumble and shake, and they charged him with the task of finding the orb and returning it to them without delay. The consequence if he failed would be the destruction of the tribe, the details of which Shtaaa revealed to Thoiink by touching a finger to his forehead. The young Zingaloo saw exactly how it would happen: the gods would send rain that would raise the river and flood the village, after which they would send fire from the sacred volcano Bazoot to pour down over the jungle, and then they'd crack open the earth and chase the tribe into the chasm with water on one side and fire on the other, closing it upon them forevermore. They would burn and wash and collapse away any evidence that the Zingaloo ever existed. Thoiink alone could save them, but only if he was as selfless as Ubwoop had been selfish. Then the column of fire rose again, and the gods were gone."

"How utterly Biblical," Croom said slyly.

"Needless to say, Thoiink was terrified. He ran back to the village and told the elders what was bound to happen if he didn't find Ubwoop and retrieve the orb, and how the tribe would be punished for the old shaman's selfishness. The villagers were convinced he'd eaten the wrong berries and hallucinated this cataclysmic vision, but Thoiink believed whole-heartedly what the gods had told him. He couldn't allow his people to perish, even if they didn't heed his message. So he set out on his own, wandering the jungle for signs of the spirit-man and his orb in all the regions he'd been rumored to exist. Finally, he came upon Ubwoop sleeping in the hollowed-out trunk of a Waliki tree with the orb cradled in his arms. He was no spirit; he was a real man, as wizened and sun-wrinkled as a raisin. Thoiink woke him gently and explained to him the terrible destruction of which the gods had warned him. But living on his own in the jungle for so long had made Ubwoop a tad insane."

Croom nodded as if he understood all too well. "It happens to the best of us."

"The shaman was so smitten with his own immortality," Bombfell continued, "that he refused to give back the orb, even if the Zingaloo would be destroyed as a result. So rather than asking a second time, Thoiink simply snatched it out of the old man's hands, turned, and ran as fast as he could through the jungle, leaving Ubwoop cursing and hollering at the base of the tree. He was now nearly three hundred years old, too aged and too frail to give chase without tripping on his beard, and once the orb was out of his possession, he could no longer survive. He fell to the jungle floor and turned to dust."

"Gadzooks!" Croom exclaimed. "This is getting exciting, isn't it?"

Bombfell grinned. "I thought you might like it."

"I wasn't certain I would," Croom said. "But I'm eager to hear what happens next!"

So Bombfell went on. "Thoiink carried the orb back to the village and said his hellos to the star-gods, hoping they'd hear his voice and return to reclaim their gift. Instead, the clouds closed down over the jungle and the punishing rains began. When he explained to his tribe that this was the beginning of the end, they laughed and told him that it rained all the time in the jungle. But on the second day, when the river began to slip its banks, they realized this was no ordinary jungle shower. And when the fire began falling in spiteful spewings from Bazoot, the Zingaloo knew they were in real danger from the gods, all thanks to Ubwoop's selfish scheming. They finally saw reason in Thoiink's message."

"And all it took to change their minds was a little flood and a spot of fire," Croom said. "Typical."

"Thoiink wasn't certain how much time he had left to save his tribe. He fretted over how he would deliver the orb to the star-gods to keep them from visiting their full wrath upon the village. Then all at once, the image of their fiery column flashed in his vision; if gods had ridden a blazing column to reach the Zingaloo, surely the Zingaloo could ride a similar column to reach the gods. So he holed up in a cave, and he toiled night and day until he created a structure he felt just might work for such a task: a coned cylinder that could ride on a stream of fire and carry him to the stars."

"Hold your galloping horses, Horatio," Croom said, pounding his fist on the table as it all developed like a photograph in his brain. "You're telling me an ancient tribesman built himself a rocket to return a magical orb to his gods?"

Bombfell smiled. "According to the myth, that's *exactly* what happened."

"Preposterous!" Croom laughed.

"But you've been fine with everything up until this point..." Bombfell pointed out.

"Well, it's a bit of a stretch, even for a myth," Croom admitted. "But yes. I'm good with everything up until the rocket."

"Then let me finish the story, and you can judge the whole thing instead."

"Sorry," Croom said sheepishly. "Please, keep going."

"So Thoiink had his column, but where would he find fire to send it sailing into the sky to reach the heavens? Bazoot was rumbling and belching in advance of the impending eruption...he supposed that if he could ride the powerful vapor streams the volcano was exhaling, he might travel to the sky quite rapidly and return the orb. So he loaded his column onto a canoe and made the treacherous, rapid-laden ride down the now-rushing Sarabezi, and he wandered his way into the heart of Bazoot's caldera, wandering through the roiling volcano as it grew angrier and angrier, until he found a portal that would aim him toward the stars, and a jet that aligned with it as closely as possible. From there, he launched, and the rocket could be seen by the entire village as it rode the stream into the heavens, off into the distance, just above the mountain peaks as the rains slowed and the clouds began to part. A small shimmer that hung at the bottom of the sky was their signal that the task had been completed: the orb had been returned to the gods. The rain stopped altogether, Bazoot slowed his eruption until it was nothing but steam, and the tribe received their salvation."

"And Thoiink?" Croom asked with great animation. "What became of that brave and clever Zingaloo savior?"

"According to the story, he was welcomed by the gods for his altruisim and granted the eternal life promised by the orb." Bombfell closed his eyes and bowed his head like a stage actor who'd just finished his final monologue. "And *scene*."

Croom applauded and cheered his friend's performance. "A wonderful story, if more than a little familiar!"

Bombfell's eyes snapped upward. "Familiar, Simeon?"

"You know very well that nearly every culture on Earth has a salvation myth, Horatio," Croom reminded him. "This one isn't terribly different from the others. Exciting, certainly, and the rocket is a mind-boggling twist, but...not terribly different, no."

"Ah, but it is." Bombfell folded his hands on the table. "There are those who believe that the story more than a myth, my friend. Some believe the orb was a genuine artifact of the Zingaloo culture, carried not by a mythological figure who became a god, but by a member of the tribe who believed so deeply in his gods' wrath, he sacrificed his life in an attempt to spare his fellow tribesmen. His story simply became a myth afterward."

"And they believe he actually set this artifact somewhere the sky?" Croom scoffed.

"Not somewhere in the sky," Bombfell corrected him. "Somewhere atop a mountainous tract called Heavencrest that surrounds the Sarabezi River, high enough to be mistaken for a celestial object when viewed under the proper conditions..."

Croom picked up the thread quite easily from there. "...where it would shine in the full light of day, to be seen hovering below the sun by an ancient tribe filled with superstitious worship of star-gods." The pieces were finally coming together.

"Yes!" Bombfell cheered. "You see the possibility of it now, don't you?"

"I believe I'm beginning to."

"Of course, two thousand years and much overgrowth of the Sarabezi mountaintop jungle later, the star isn't likely to shine in any sort of light to lead us to its whereabouts. However..." Bombfell reached into a satchel that hung on his chair beneath his suit coat and removed a stone tablet the size of a shirt box. "Upon his deathbed, Twill bequeathed this little beauty to me in hopes that I could divine its significance. I believe with a generous serving of your help, I can do just that."

"Do you, now?" Croom intoned. Bombfell handed him the tablet as his eyes crept along the shape of it, from edge to edge, from side to center, from front to back to front once more. It was surprisingly light for something so solid, peppered with strange symbols and a scattering of holes in various shapes and sizes, as if stone-eating moths had snacked on it like a cardigan through the millennia.

"I do indeed," Bombfell affirmed. "That little prize is somewhere in the mountains surrounding the Sarabezi, and this tablet is key in figuring out where. I'm determined to locate it, to prove that the life work of Eddington Twill wasn't in vain." Bombfell made serious, soulful eyes at Croom. "But I need your help, Simeon, dear friend. You're the only other explorer I know who's intrepid enough to trudge through the jungle with me in search of an object like this, and who's insightful enough to interpret the mysteries of an extinct culture in order to lead us there."

Croom couldn't be certain whether Bombfell had said "intrepid" or "stupid," but it made no difference; by now, Croom's explorer imagination had begun humming like an engine with a sharp new key sunk into its ignition switch.

It wasn't without its limitations, however.

"You're asking me to believe that some rube in an ancient tropical tribe designed a rocket made of stone that could ride volcanic plumes into the sky over two millennia ago so he could deposit a jeweled orb onto a mountain top to appease his gods, and that we should go traipsing along

the Sarabezi in hopes of finding it? Absurd!" Croom hardly remembered that the majority of their adventures began
with a similar exclamation.

"Isn't it, though?" Bombfell agreed.

"It truly is— utterly and entirely!"

Bombfell wrung his hands. "So you're up for it, then?"

Croom's vision went slack as he pictured the steam
and the buzz of the jungle simmering around him while
he slashed a path with his trusty machete, Doris (and yes,
his machete had a name—a woman's name, at that), and a
flask full of Goodsense swinging from his hip. "Well, of
course I am!"

"Of course you're *not*," said a feminine voice as it
joined the conversation.

Croom and Bombfell shared a look of thorough confusion.

"I don't think I'm drunk enough for my voice to sound
that pretty," Bombfell said.

Croom scratched his head. "And I usually don't dis-
agree with myself before sunrise..."

"Ahem, gentlemen."

She appeared at the table like a shadow cast by the
moon through the plate-glass window. Though her ethe-
real loveliness lent weight to the theory that she might be
something illusory, her perfect dimensions said she was
anything but.

"How...how did you get in here?" Bombfell stam-
mered, thrown by both her sudden, silent presence in the
bar and her breathtaking beauty. "Murphy locks the door
from the outside."

The woman held her hands behind her back as if she
were hiding a secret there. "I have a hairpin and nimble
fingers from years of counted cross-stitch taught to me by

my grandmother. Also: the lock on the front door isn't the sturdiest of contraptions. The story wrote its own conclusion."

Bombfell practically applauded. "Well done then, Miss. *Bravisse!*"

She was hardly impressed by this undue praise, or by Bombfell's gaze as it wandered the height and breadth of her. Her skin had the pristine luster of polished bone, as if she'd been set aside in a drawer for safe keeping until this very moment; her face was a perfect upside-down teardrop nested in a crown of shining black hair that slipped down her cheeks and ended in a sharp angle at her chin. And the mysterious grace and purposeful poise with which she carried her elegant form suggested either that she was profoundly studied in ballet, or was skilled in the danger-sport of knife-throwing, or was practiced in the art of slipping through a coat hanger without having to hold her breath.

That she was a perfect combination of all three was a hidden truth few knew first-hand.

Croom just so happened to be on the short list.

Regardless of all this wonder, she was to him simply his trustworthy, dependable assistant Nebula Everhope, fetcher of coffee and sharpener of pencils.

"Tracked me down again, Neb," Croom said as he shook the final drops of bourbon from his glass. "You're getting sharp at this Let's Find Simeon game."

His condescension set Nebula's teeth on edge. "Given that there are only three possibilities for your whereabouts at any given time—namely, the museum, your flat, or this *wondrous* establishment—and considering that you're rarely at the first two after seven p.m., there's really no game about it at all. It's simply a foregone conclusion."

Croom's lower lip stuck out like a window sill. "You're no fun."

"And you're lucky I had that hairpin."

Bombfell laughed like a crack of thunder to see his blustering friend put in his place so deftly as his eyes drank in the absolute vision before him. But this woman was more than just a vision; she was a mind and a spirit beyond compare, a bombshell genius who possessed myriad skills about which she spoke only when absolutely necessary. And she used them almost exclusively in the service of cleaning up Croom's overbearing, lunk-headed messes... and yet he never seemed to realize how lucky he was to have such a colleague.

"Simeon...aren't you going to introduce me to this raven-haired splendor?" Bombfell purred. "The one with the electric wit and the tongue to match..."

"I'd appreciate it greatly if you refrained from speaking about my tongue," Nebula said, without so much as a smirk.

The gravity of her tone told Bombfell that she wasn't making a request; she was issuing a command. "Yes ma'am," he said, though the lilt in his words indicated that he would probably be unable to keep his promise.

Croom intervened to break the tension—or to heighten it, depending upon whose perspective the conversation was viewed from. "Horatio Bombfell, this is Nebula Everhope; she makes sure I appear as polished and presentable as the Hydewhite Museum trustees believe me to be. Nebula, this is Horatio Bombfell, adventure-seeker, treasure-hunter, and explorer extraordinaire of lost worlds, second only to myself in experiences of derring-do."

"Nebula," Bombfell said, "named for the very heavens

themselves...and rightly so," His words became lost in a fascinated whisper near the end.

Nebula wasn't nearly as fascinated with Bombfell in return. "Actually, a nebula is an ionized plasma cloud, merely a *part* of the heavens as you so carelessly call them...but I'm sure that's what you meant."

"Charmed and delighted to make your acquaintance, Miss Everhope," Bombfell said as he held out his hand.

"Wary and disappointed to make yours, Mr. Bombfell," Nebula countered as she refused to take it.

"Is there a reason you've come to break up my reunion with my oldest living friend, Neb?" Croom asked. "We were just getting started."

Nebula's brow kinked. "Has it occurred to you at any point during the evening that you're due at the museum at eight a.m. tomorrow to deliver your lecture about the growing disregard for the significance of ancient culture and its far-reaching impact on contemporary anthropology?"

Croom's mustache practically curled at the reminder. "Thunderball! I forgot about that entirely."

"I wouldn't be here to carry you home if you'd remembered."

"No. You probably wouldn't be." He smiled broadly.

Bombfell studied Nebula's structure as if he recognized something familiar in her. "Your almond eyes slanting ever so slightly upward...your wide, delicate jaw...your high-set cheekbones. Do I detect islander heritage?"

It wasn't just her tongue now; Nebula wasn't comfortable with him describing any part of her at all. "You may impress your drinking buddy here with your intellectual savvy and your powers of deduction, but I'm not yours for decrypting, Mr. Bombfell."

"It's *Dr.* Bombfell, actually."

"Actually, it's inconsequential. The presentation is in..." She gazed at the watch encircling her delicate wrist. It practically floated about the bone, as if in orbit. "...four hours, Simeon, at which time you'll need to be entirely sober and far more presentable than you currently are. And for that, you'll require sleep, a new shirt, and a fresh pair of slacks." She sniffed the vile current of alcohol-steeped air that wafted from the surface of him. "And a torrid encounter with an open fire hydrant to remove that stench. You reek of vagrant."

"I've had a rousing night of rolling around on this barroom floor!" Croom sang.

"You might want to sound less proud of that."

"Horatio was just telling me about a possible opportunity for adventure..." Croom cast curious, still-interested eyes in Bombfell's direction.

"Was he? How irresponsible of him."

Bombfell's laughter boomed through the bar like a bass drum. "What fire she has—what zest!"

Nebula preferred not to be referenced by sentiments such as this, and she certainly didn't appreciate being spoken about as if she wasn't in the room. "While Dr. Bombfell's sudden appearance in Haven City may be a rollicking good time for him, it's an extraordinary inconvenience for you, Simeon. You do realize that the board of trustees will be present to determine their allocations to the Vanished Civilizations, Mythical Creatures, and Artifacts of Incredible Antiquity wing, don't you? Our entire budget hinges on you."

The pressure of this had been building on Croom for several months, which was likely why a drunk and disorderly reunion with an old friend at the eleventh hour had sounded like such a fantastic idea. He tilted confidently in his chair. "Bah! I could charm the purse strings loose on those stodgy old curmudgeons even twice as drunk as I am at the moment." The chair teetered on its two back feet, and Croom put his dual sense of agility and balance to fine use as he held form, his arms nearly as wide open as his eyes. The chair hung there in a continuation of his grand acrobatic display from earlier. Then physics asserted itself as it was bound to do, and the chair finished its tipping. Croom fell flat on his back on Murphy's floor, a six-legged beast with beer on his wingtips, turned belly-up for a disappointed audience of two. "Oof."

Nebula sighed. "Yes, precisely. Oof."

"Correct me if I'm wrong, but wouldn't the addition of a new and decidedly mysterious artifact actually serve to help your cause?" Bombfell asked presumptuously, with an opportunistic gleam in his eye.

"Your manipulations aren't welcome in this conversation," Nebula insisted. "Simeon needs his wits about him, and far fewer stains on his clothes in order to present the sharp-edged image the board expects, and he has precious little time left to attain that." She crouched at Croom's side and tugged on his elbow, helping him first to his hands and knees, and then to his feet as he rose, staggered, and leaned on the table for much-needed support.

Bombfell's face fell slack. "I'm merely suggesting that a new adventure could breathe fresh life into your museum, my dear. Surely you can see the reason in this." Then he made the gravest mistake of the entire evening: he lay his hand on top of hers where it rested on the table.

Nebula's eye twitched.

"Perhaps we should get a few things straight, Dr. Bombfell," she said calmly yet assertively. "Firstly, I am not your 'dear'...I am not your *anything*, in fact, though I'm incredibly close to becoming your adversary. Secondly: I am not to be touched by you for any cause other than to extinguish me if for some reason I happen to catch fire. And even then, you should ask first. I might prefer the flames."

"Such a pistol!" Bombfell laughed, though his hand remained where it was.

Placing her free hand upon his, Nebula pinched the fat pad of flesh between his thumb and forefinger ever so lightly. Though her touch was delicate and controlled, Bombfell's face seized, locking into a veneer of excruciating ache and slack-jawed surprise as an agonizing bolt of pain rose from his hand, passed through his arm, and worked its way into his neck. "If I were to squeeze just a bit harder, you would lose the vision in your left eye—permanently. So in summary: you'll either call me Miss Everhope and keep your hands to yourself, or you should prepare to invest in a fashionable assortment of eye patches and monocles. Do I make myself clear?"

Bombfell's cheek shuddered. "Like the summer winds across the Mbigo desert, Miss Everhope." His voice was flush with pain.

"Perfect," Nebula said, finally offering a smile as she released his hand. "Let's try to remember that from now on."

"She's right, Horatio," Croom said, finishing their terse exchange. "I have neither the time nor the space in my life for a new adventure at the moment." He cracked his neck, and then his back, and then his shoulders. Then he stretched his longish arms far above his head for good measure. "There are scant hours left to prepare for impressing the curmudgeons with my silver-throated charm and my dazzling eyebrow choreography." He waggled his brows for dramatic effect, though no one bothered to notice.

"I understand," Bombfell said, feigning reluctant acceptance. "Far be it from me to keep a man from his museum in favor of a boisterous adventure in the jungle that could very well result in the discovery of a relic that until now has been believed to live only in an ancient tribal myth."

Croom felt the last of his drunken stupor diminish as Bombfell spoke. "You actually believe there's something out there, don't you?

Bombfell rested his hand over his heart, now that the searing pain had subsided and he could move it again. "There is *always* something out there, Simeon. Who would know that better than we?"

It was the motto they had lived by for nearly their entire lives.

"Take the tablet," Bombfell implored, "and consider the opportunity before us. But don't take too long; I've begun making travel arrangements that can't be reversed, and it would be a far less enjoyable endeavor without you."

"Another reason you've shown up at this very moment, I presume?" Croom postulated. "To prevent me from thinking about it too much before answering and talking myself out of it?"

Bombfell practically blushed. "Men of our ilk tend to make the most exhilarating decisions during moments of haste, I find."

Croom scooped up the stone slab as Nebula gathered his jacket. "Your offer is enticing, Horatio. But I warn you that my days of adventure are past me now."

"Or perhaps they're yet ahead of you." Bombfell's smile drew down into a certain, satisfied grin, like a latch being fastened. "I'll expect an answer tomorrow." He checked his pocket watch and realized his error. "Make that later today."

Nebula guided a starry-eyed Simeon Croom to the door. "You'll be lucky if you get his 'no' by telephone, Dr. Bombfell," she said. "Goodnight."

"A pleasure to meet you, my...er, Miss Everhope," Bombfell called out behind them as they exited Murphy's.

Croom walked in a zigzag along the curb while Nebula leaned into him to keep him from tipping over into the street. "You seem cranky, Neb. Did your cat run away again?"

"No, Simeon," she huffed, irritated that she had to explain it to him yet again. "It's four thirty a.m., and we have a presentation that you haven't even worked through yet. You're half-drunk and half-asleep, and our very livelihoods at the museum depend upon you maintaining your stablity and common sense."

"Sounds like a typical day to me."

"Well, how about this to justify my anger, then: I don't like your friend. He has lizard eyes, his hands feel like snow, and it seems as if everything he says is designed to give him some sort of advantage over whomever he's speaking to."

There had been a clattering laugh in the back of Croom's throat just waiting for Nebula to make her assessment. "Oh, Horatio is harmless. He just wants us to have one last adventure for old times' sake."

Nebula's head swung, sending Simeon's nose the scent of cherry blossoms. "You have *new* times' sake to keep ahead of, Simeon, and a lifetime of work that hangs in the balance for you. You'd best hope you can be ready to persuade the board to increase their funding for the wing, or we'll be cooked for sure."

Croom smiled at her insistence, like a child with a toy he'd forgotten to cherish until that very moment. "Oh, Neb. Never to worry. You know I always come through in a clutch."

Nebula clucked. "Only because you have me working the wheel. And the brakes."

Croom's finger waved insistently in the air between them. "You forget how much power I yield...my ever-persuasive *froonge de cloupard,* as the French call it."

"Those aren't real words, Simeon."

"They aren't?" Croom dropped into the passenger seat and pondered. "Not even in French?"

Nebula was thoroughly confounded that such a brilliant man could be so unaware of his own limitations. She could do little more than shake her lovely, knowing head and wonder how he managed to keep his shoes tied. "Especially not in French," she said.

"That should be the next language I acquire, then," Croom laughed.

The engine started with a little kick as Nebula twisted the key. "I'll add it to your schedule, right after 'Sober up considerably' but before 'Stop agreeing to ridiculous excursions with questionable friends.'"

Croom laughed even louder as she pulled away from the curb and drove him home. "Does anyone know me better than you, Neb?"

Nebula sighed. "For the sake of everyone else's sanity, I certainly hope not."

THREE

Simeon Croom was standing surprisingly upright for the most part, not because he wanted to, but because the lectern upon which he leaned wouldn't allow him to do otherwise. His shirt was impeccably starched and pressed, his coffee-colored suit coat wrinkle-free, and his dusty-brown vest tautly-buttoned against his flat belly. The pleats in his pant legs were so straight and crisp, they could have been considered origami. And the knot in his russet tie had the privilege of being Windsored in a way that few ties had ever had, courtesy of Nebula Everhope's deft handiwork. Yet for all of his linear precision, there was something entirely crooked about him, as if he'd been wrestled into his clothes, and in turn, forced into the improbable shape of an explorer-turned-museum lecturer. It made him realize even more distinctly how little adventure there really was in his life anymore.

He had chosen to forgo sleep before the presentation in favor of engaging in two hours of Kasig, an ancient Sawilian technique used for focused relaxation, during which a precisely-measured balance of deep-diaphragm humming and staring into an open candle flame (or in this case, an exposed light bulb filament) served to adjust his circadian rhythms, thus fooling his body into believing it had just spent a full eight hours in restful sleep. And as a failsafe, he'd consumed an incredible quantity of black coffee, brewed by the ever-forethoughtful Nebula to a strength only recently approved by food scientists as safe for human consumption.

And yet, he still felt as if he'd been dragged along behind a city bus while chewing on a raccoon.

Seated before him in the Hydewhite Museum for the Preservation of Uncommon Artifacts auditorium and lecture hall were the seven stoic officers from the board of trustees. They were monolithic, stiff and stone-faced, their collective glare challenging Croom to make a misstep, or express an opinion they didn't agree with, or give them even a slip of a reason to dismiss his claims that his wing of the museum was in more dire need of new funding than were the other departments in order to bring a fresh wave of visitors. It was an annual thing, this begging for scraps and salvage, though in the decade he'd held the position he'd never quite seen the reason for it. In his own world view, arguing that vanishing cultures and mythical creatures and items of great antiquity were worth investing in was like trying to put stockings on an ostrich: futile, humiliating, and ultimately unnecessary, even if the ostrich did end up looking quite fetching when all was said and done. Fewer things were more appropriate in a museum than articles of physical evidence that illuminated the grand, mysterious wonders of the world and gave voice to extinct peoples whose cultures had disappeared hundreds of years earlier. And yet somehow, Croom felt as though he were explaining this to the board for the first time, every time. Of all the arcane cultures he'd encountered in his years of discovery, the culture of the museum bureaucrat was by far the most perplexing.

And the most obstinate.

Nebula stood nearby to his left, poised and ready to step forward and hoist him back to his feet by his coattails in a most practiced yet casual manner, should his lack of sleep overtake him and crumple him like a paper cup. Knowing he'd be in no shape to compose his thoughts beforehand, she'd prepared a three-page statement and arranged a compelling slideshow that highlighted the more exciting displays in the wing.

Croom stared at her typewritten notes resting on the lectern. Even her typewriting had a loveliness about it, as if the letters on the keys were eager to please her and had all lined up more precisely under her stroke than they would have for anyone else using the same machine. Her thoughts were as clear and concise as ever, and her ideas were exactly what the board wanted to hear. But Croom had something even more compelling hidden beneath the papers, covered almost entirely by them, though its rough, ruddy edges peeked out all along the margins. It was the tablet Bombfell had given him, a final prospect for exploration and adventure, and it made him feel as if he'd found a stray ticket in his pocket that would guarantee him one last ride along the midway before the carnival that had been his life as an explorer dropped its banner and closed down forever.

Croom scanned the lemon-puckered faces of the officers and pushed Nebula's notes aside as he began. "My esteemed colleagues and officers of the board of trustees of the Hydewhite Museum for the Preservation of Uncommon Artifacts," he announced, squinting at the harsh glow streaming in through the auditorium skylight. "I ask you on this good and painfully sunny morning: what is it that draws people to exhibits such as these, in a museum such as ours?"

The officers shifted and grunted as a single unit. It was their typical response for moments when Croom spoke off-the-cuff and asked pondering, rhetorical questions of them. This year, they offered no answer, allowing him instead to trim three seconds of their frustrated guessing out of the presentation and get right to the heart of matters.

"Do they come to see a dashing ex-adventurer recount his heroic exploits in the manner of a matinee idol reliving his glory days before the camera? Probably, yes...that's a thing people like, usually. Do they come for the free coffee and crullers in the lobby? Quite possibly...they are very good crullers, and I make it a point to say so every time I have one. Do they come to walk the endless halls of academic heritage and dwell among remarkable archaeological spectacles they would never see anywhere else? I suppose they do...sometimes, maybe?" Croom's eyes slid toward the back of the room. "I don't remember where I was going with this."

One of Nebula's wondrous abilities was speaking through her nostrils instead of her mouth, which allowed her to remind Croom of just what his purpose there was. "You were about to grovel for the money that we so desperately need..."

"Ah, yes...the funding." Even he wasn't certain he'd arrive at the proper conclusion when he started speaking. But it all came together nicely in his head now that his severe caffeine consumption had taken control.

He picked up the tablet and held it aloft. "What good does having a storehouse of artifacts do us if there are cultures we've yet to observe, if there are treasures we've yet to behold, if there are sights and sounds and curiosities still awaiting discovery somewhere out there in all the hidden hollows of the world?"

A single eyebrow arched in impatient irritation by a member of the board seemed to issue an audible squeak.

"I have an opportunity to travel to the jungle surrounding the Sarabezi River and possibly recover an artifact long-believed to be just an element in a story from the relatively unstudied Zingaloo tribe, a people who vanished two thousand years ago, presumably supplanted by the other tribes in the region. I can claim this item for the museum and spark new interest in antiquities, which will in turn bring a new channel of visitors flowing through these halls to fill the coffers for all of our benefit. I believe, gentlemen, that for the first time since I arrived at Hydewhite to oversee this wing, I can actually make us money." He was surprised that it sounded so composed and supremely well-thought-out, considering he hadn't even made the decision to go with Bombfell until the moment he said it aloud.

"Simeon, what are you doing?" Nebula asked him, her ventriloquistic nostrils flaring. "This isn't what the presentation is for!"

"On the contrary, Neb," he whispered back through his ears, a skill he was revealing to her for the first time that very moment. "This is *exactly* what it's for."

He held back a smile that would make him seem too eager and kept his renewed vigor in careful check. "Now, of course, this expedition will be somewhat costly...I'm not overly familiar with the region, but I would imagine the areas are treacherous and difficult to reach. What I'll need from you is the chance to take the voyage—to make the journey to the Sarabezi and use this stone tablet, which my good friend Dr. Horatio Bombfell and his mentor Dr. Eddington Twill both believe reveal the location of the artifact, something they call the Treasure Star." Croom cleared his throat and presented his most perfect, polished smile as he clicked the power switch on the slide projector. The enormous image of a grand, shimmering gold vase appeared on the screen behind him. He turned to glance and recoiled at how large and shiny it was, even in a photograph. "Good lord! That's huge..."

Nebula groaned through her nose.

"This...isn't actually the Treasure Star...nobody has seen it, as far as I know. It's an object from the mythology of a tribe that no longer exists, after all." He realized that his patter might be working against him now, and he changed tack, in that *froonge de cloupard* way he had. "But I'm sure it's wonderful, too."

There was silence in the crowd.

"And in order to afford this expedition, I'll need the grant that I've come here to beg you for. The full amount."

For the first time ever, Croom heard the officers of the Hydewhite board of trustees laugh...but it wasn't a good-natured, agreeable laughter; it was more the sort of laughter that comes when one says something ridiculous to people who are already entirely too familiar with hearing similar ridiculous things coming from one's mouth.

"Why don't you just ask for the contents of the gift shop till, the snack bar coffee machine, and the entire petty cash fund while you're at it?" asked Roderick Fulk, president of the board and the most pinched of the officers. "You could clean us out entirely in one felled swoop."

"Well...if you're offering, I wouldn't say no to that, either."

Fulk's head tilted so far back, he was at risk of having moths fly into his nostrils. "You're no more deserving of this sort of consideration than any other department head in the museum."

His derision was accompanied by a sneer that Croom often longed to smooth out with a solid haymaker to Fulk's ever-so-uppity nose, which he would have likely followed through with today had the man been within punching distance. Instead, he blinked twice, held his fists at his sides, and said, "Unless they're willing to risk life and limb to bring Hydewhite the sort of acclaim and prominence it hasn't enjoyed in years, then yes...I absolutely *am* more deserving. And more qualified." It wasn't nearly as satisfying as a haymaker, but in the crusty world of academia, it would have to suffice. "And I'm more handsome, too."

"What does that have to do with anything?" Fulk fumed.

"Nothing. I just felt like maybe it wasn't being appreciated as much as usual. That's all."

Nebula's blood boiled to hear him speak so distastefully to the board. She only hoped they would realize his truculence was the result of a night with Phineas Goodsense, write it off as more Croomian nonsense, and allow him to keep his job. But extra funding seemed an improbability at this point.

The officers may have been put off by Croom's smug confidence, but his line of thinking was beyond reproach, an occurrence they seldom expected when in his presence. They had no choice but to consider his proposal. So they turned their backs to the lectern like a council of hunched, bitter owls and leaned their heads together to discuss this most unexpected twist in their decision-making process.

"Negotiating has never been your strong suit, Simeon," Nebula said, using the full vocal power of her open mouth this time, though she said it quietly enough that only the two of them could hear. "You know your best approach has always been to bow your head and show respect to the natives as you step onto their island."

"This is my island too, Neb. Surely I can shake my spear a little and rile the elders if my cause is just."

"Unless your 'cause is just' to gallivant across the globe so that you and your incredibly untrustworthy friend can play explorers one last time."

Croom chuckled at the thought of it. "If the elders are willing, then..."

Nebula was too incensed for island metaphors now. "You're being too brusque...too cocksure. It'll put them on the defensive at the very least, and make them distrust your intentions at the very most."

"Or, with one well-delivered stroke, I could secure long-term funding for the wing, garner a grand round of glory for the museum, and have another dose of the adventure I seem to have misplaced in my life, Neb," Croom explained, making it sound more rational than perhaps it should have. "Doesn't that solve the entire situation in the most favorable manner possible for all involved?"

In a small and unexpectedly pensive way, Nebula now understood where he was aiming his figurative spear. But with the livelihoods of the entire department hanging in the balance, she couldn't bring herself to agree that it was worth risking the ire of the officers by letting it fly. "Be that as it may, you're putting the jobs of everyone who works here in unnecessary peril."

Croom was no stranger to unnecessary peril, and this was a far cry from that. "'Everyone' would be you, me, and the man who dusts the cases and cleans fingerprints off the glass."

"His name is Gable; you should know that by now… he's worked here for seven years. There's also a woman named Olga who sweeps the floors, in case you've forgotten."

"Ah yes…Olga. She's so quiet, I forget she's even there sometimes."

"Actually, she's only there at night, after we leave."

"That would explain it." Croom winked in a way that made Nebula want to smash him in the face with a bag of nickels. Fortunately for him, she didn't have one handy.

The officers turned unceremoniously and faced Croom and Nebula and the lectern, which was now simply a prop upon which Croom leaned rakishly as he loosened his russet Windsor and opened his mind further to the idea of a spirited roll in the jungle in search of the Treasure Star. "So gentlemen…has my proposal piqued your interest in this new artifact, thereby cracking the combination to your safe? I could always juggle fiery batons while doing backflips up the colonnade if it would help you see things my way." He pulled a cigarette lighter from his vest and gave the wheel a crafty flick.

Nebula could feel her fingernails press into her palms as her fists grew tighter.

"Don't even think about it, Croom," Fulk said. "The last thing we need is a repeat of your performance from last year's Christmas party."

Croom flipped the lighter in the air and caught it in his coat pocket. "Suit yourselves."

Martin Ayers, the board's second-in-command, cleared his throat and spoke in a professional yet understanding manner that Roderick Fulk seemed incapable of. "Bear in mind, Mr. Croom, that the only reason we would ever entertain such an unusual request is because we know how dearly the museum is suffering...without a dependable up-tick in attendance, we'll soon be as dead as the dinosaurs in the Cretaceous displays on the third floor."

"I understand entirely. Those things are incredibly dead."

"We could just as easily route the funding to the Un-moored Ships and Questionable Settlements wing," Fulk reminded him. He'd never been comfortable with Croom's challenges to his authority; if there were to be consent given by the board in this scenario, he would make certain it came with very definite expectations.

"I'm sure the public would clamor to see another rust-ed cannon or tattered linen sail," Croom chided, "just as much as they would to see a star plucked from the histo-ry of one of the greatest unexplored mythologies of the last two millennia." Fulk's mouth clamped shut with an audible *fwump*. Quite oppositely, the rest of the officers found their own mouths spread open in wide smiles at the soaring potential for a Hydewhite renaissance that Croom and his adventuresome nature now represented.

Nebula couldn't allow herself to release even a whisper of the laughter she held in at hearing his bluster begin to work in his favor. It would only signal him to continue in this manner, and he was taking chances that she knew better than to sanction. Even worse, he'd be much more difficult to deal with if he knew how impressed she was that his dicey improvised tactic was actually working.

"The funds are yours, Mr. Croom," Martin Ayers con-firmed.

"Wonderful—thank you, gentlemen!" Croom sang. Nebula was pleased to hear that he had at least enough common sense and social grace to be grateful for the board's decision. In years past, he'd had the nerve to ask for more than was being offered. "Wondering how likely would be that you'd double the amount if I told you there might be other artifacts to be discovered during this expedition?"

And there it was.

The board laughed again, far louder this time, thinking Croom's suggestion was an expression of good humor rather than a clumsy, toe-crunching attempt at wringing extra money out of them to make his travels a bit more comfortable, while Nebula's forehead creased in a pattern that only appeared during his more infuriating moments.

"You're lucky to be getting the original amount, Croom," Fulk barked as he departed behind the rest of the board. "Don't push your luck."

Croom glanced sidewise at Nebula and smiled from the corner of his mouth, an expression she found even more displeasing than his winking. "Never hurts to ask," he said.

Nebula reared back one of her long-clenched fists and walloped him squarely in the chest—once, twice, then three times, in rapid-fire succession. "Does it hurt now?" she asked.

Croom groaned, wondering how she managed to pack so much power in such a small, elegant hand. "Now that you mention it...yes it does." He rubbed the sore spot, wondering how extensive the bruising would be. "Quite a lot, actually."

FOUR

It was a hen's feather past sunrise the next Saturday morning when Simeon Croom and Horatio Bombfell met on the sleepy tarmac of a private airstrip located just beyond the borders of Haven City. By calling upon Bombfell's seemingly endless list of helpful connections and greasing the clandestine wheels of progress using Croom's considerable financial endowment from Hydewhite, the two were able to secure a nonstop monoplane flight to the far western coast. From there, they would board an experimental craft of which even the military wasn't aware—the chimeric blending of a plane and a dirigible that was capable of speeds and smoothness unprecedented in the field of air travel, provided by transportation heir Evelyn Alder, who was a friend and donor to Hydewhite—in hopes of flying as quickly as possible over the ocean and toward the heart of the Sarabezi, where they hoped to parachute into a secret predetermined destination to meet their guide, who would then hopefully direct their sojourn with the tablet that would, with any hope at all, reveal the location of the Treasure Star.

Their reliance on hope at every point in their voyage could not be overemphasized.

In spite of having what both thought of as a well-determined direction in which to head, there were incredible variables in the equation that neither could account for. "But aren't the variables the very heart of adventure, Simeon?" Bombfell asked over a breakfast sherry in the aerodrome lounge.

"Truly," Croom concurred, toasting his old friend with a sherry of his own design, which was really just a lager served in a sherry glass, because sherry had never been one of his numerous indulgences, and it wasn't going to become one now. "The greatest moments of our journeys together have always come when we've thrown away our compass, turned our telescope to the skies of our souls, and allowed ourselves to be guided by the stars that shone there instead."

It struck such a sweet philosophical note that Bombfell could hardly keep himself from crying out, "By the gods!" and raising his glass high above his head for Croom to meet in a grand toast. "To the advent of new exploits!"

Croom raised his glass to meet Bombfell's. "To the memory of the old ones!"

A messenger appeared at their table and leaned intrusively into the glory of their toast. "To the front office with you please, Mr. Croom!" He sounded every bit as cheerful as the two gentlemen did. "You have a visitor who insists on seeing you before you board the Grand Zephyr."

Bombfell shrugged his eyebrows. "Who even knows you're here at the moment?"

Croom closed his eyes and imagined what calamity back at the museum might have necessitated such an intervention. "There would be only one individual in possession of my schedule for the next two weeks: the one who drafted it."

"Ah...the lovely Miss Everhope, then!"

"Yes. She seems determined to find me at every indulgent instant to wring the liquor out of things, and all the fun along with it." Croom stood and drained his lager, then set his glass back on the table with a troublesome *thud*. "Back in a click, Horatio. Hold the plane for me, should they crank the propellers before I return."

"I wouldn't dream of leaving without you, Simeon," Bombfell said, signaling the waitress for a refill.

Croom made his way to the front office to find Nebula Everhope tapping her fingers on the desk, her face awash in unsurprising exasperation. "Why, hello there, Neb," he said amiably, if not genuinely. "I thought we understood that you'd stay behind to keep things running smoothly at the museum while I was gone."

"Yes, well...apparently I needed to keep things running smoothly here, too." She held up his traveler's pack, which included both the compass and the telescope he'd referenced in his reminiscences about earlier adventures with Bombfell, as well as his tool kit, his shaving kit, and his spare socks.

Croom laughed as it swung from her finger by its strap. "Wouldn't get far without that, would I? Thank you for bringing it to me."

Nebula didn't respond...nor did she move, which Croom found to be a bit troubling.

"Was there something else you needed?" he asked.

But of course there was. "I'm still not convinced that this trip is the boon you've portrayed it as, Simeon," she told him, reiterating her concerns. "It seems a tad too convenient..."

"It's six days of globe-rounding travel," Croom reminded her, "followed by another three days on a river, winding through a jungle, leading to a mountain range, to find a relic deposited there most likely by volcano-assisted flight. How exactly does this sound convenient to you?"

"I do realize all of that," Nebula assured him. "I was the one who typed your itinerary. That's not the kind of convenient I mean, and you know it."

"Think of the good this trip could do for the museum, Neb."

"Is that why you're really doing this, Simeon – for the museum?"

Croom's chagrin at his double-loaded agenda would hardly allow him to look at her as he answered, so he stared at the clean, white crescent moons of his fingernails instead. "By and large."

"How thoroughly odd, considering you'd never even mentioned an interest in traveling on behalf of Hydewhite to collect new treasures before your overwhelmingly suspect friend appeared like a muse from on high to inspire you."

Croom shrugged. "Hydewhite has never asked me to, profitable though it would be for them. And I honestly had thought my adventuring days were behind me. But I imagine even without Horatio's prodding, I would have come to the same conclusion on my own eventually."

"And what conclusion is that?" Bombfell sauntered their way with his sherry glass sloshing about like a goldfish bowl on a roller coaster.

"I was just reminding Nebula how beneficial this new adventure will be for the museum," Croom said confidently. "One of their very own traipsing around the world to make new discoveries and all that."

"A public relations heyday!" Bombfell encouraged. "Think of the headlines! Think of the publicity!"

He laughed a dragon's breath of fumes into Nebula's unsuspecting nose. "Do you ever drink anything that doesn't contain alcohol, Dr. Bombfell?" she asked.

Bombfell slurped his sherry. "Not if I can help it."

"It will be worth all the trouble, Neb," Croom reassured her, for all the good it did. "I promise you. We'll just shuttle ourselves to the Sarabezi, snatch up the Treasure Star, and carry it back to the museum—won't we, Horatio?"

Bombfell cheered emphatically. "As long as we have your expertise by which to read the map, we'll be right as rain!"

"Er...but it was always you who read the maps," Croom reminded him. "It's why I gave you the nickname 'Old MapDonald'...isn't it?" He was suddenly less than certain about this.

"No," Bombfell insisted, "I distinctly remember you carrying the atlas close to your heart as if it were...your personal diary..." His active memory seemed to hastily dispel that image. "Oh dear. That wasn't you, was it?"

"No. It wasn't."

"Well, it certainly wasn't me."

"Then to whom did I give the nickname?" Croom wondered. "Seems too clever to have gone to waste..."

"So neither of you know how to navigate by map—this is what you're realizing only moments before you head off into the wilds of the Sarabezi to find an artifact that might not actually exist?" Nebula felt the tension gathering in her neck.

Croom couldn't be fazed. "Well, we always hired guides."

"Yes!" Bombfell cried out. "And we have this time, too."

"There, Neb—you see?" Croom said smugly. "No reason for worry; we have a guide."

Nebula grimaced. "And does this guide know how to get you to a location that you haven't even identified yet, or are you going to wander up one side of the jungle and down the other hoping he instinctively knows where to find a relic that might not even exist?"

Bombfell said. "I...don't properly know, when you put it that way."

"We do have the tablet," Croom said, as if it were any help at all.

"Yes!" Bombfell erupted. "The tablet!"

"And that tells you what, exactly?" Nebula asked.

"Uh..." Croom said quietly. "Still working on that."

There were so many embarrassed eyes darting around in front of her, Nebula could hardly track the movement of any of them. "I thought as much."

Croom and Bombfell shared a single awkward look between them. But one was plenty. "Is she always this pleasant before noon?" Bombfell asked.

"No," Croom replied sincerely. "Sometimes she's in a bad mood."

Nebula turned the telephone on the desk toward her and dialed with great pressure and considerable aggravation. "May I speak to Gilda Rhone, please?"

Croom leaned in to Bombfell conspiratorially. "Gilda is the librarian at the museum."

Bombfell slurped his sherry. "Aha! Is she as lovely as her melodic name suggests?"

Croom watched Nebula twist the phone cord around her finger, noticing she'd dressed for the occasion, in her finely-fitted Tally Ho trousers, her cream-colored collared shirt with a chocolate-brown sash wrapped in a tidy X over her chest and pinned at the center, and her cross-shoulder carrying pack. Even when dressed this way, like a competitor in a fox hunt, she was a vision to behold. "She's no Nebula Everhope," he said. "That's for certain."

Bombfell's eyebrows waggled like puppets. "Is there a fire burning in that adventuresome heart for a lovely and exotic though somewhat self-righteous museum assistant, Simeon? An almond-eyed beauty with skin of bone and hair of night?"

"What? No. I mean…" Croom shook off his stupor at once. "No?"

It didn't seem a definitive answer to either of them.

Bombfell deigned to agree, though he saw much more there than Croom was willing to speak of. "Well, as long as you're certain."

Nebula heard nothing of what they said. "Gilda? It's Nebula. Can you please arrange for a docent from Ships and Settlements to cover my absence for the next ten days? Yes…I was supposed to fill in for Simeon while he was gone, but it appears that I'm needed on his little excursion." Her eyes slid toward the two increasingly contrite men in front of her. "It turns out they need a navigator… neither one knows how to read a map." Gilda's laughter came crackling through the earpiece, while Nebula did an admirable job resisting the urge to join her. "We'll catch up when I get back, Gil. Thanks for helping me out." She hung up the phone and stared into Croom's blushing face. "All settled. I'm coming with you…because I *do* know how to read a map."

"But you didn't even pack for this," Croom reminded her.

Nebula swung a small valise onto the counter. "Oh, didn't I?"

Bombfell was far more impressed than Croom was. "Her efficiency in anticipating your missteps is incredible!"

Nebula finally allowed herself to accept one of Bombfell's compliments. "At least someone appreciates that." She felt as though she needed a bath as soon as she said it. Then she pulled her valise from the counter, handed Croom his pack, and took quick, confident steps toward the tarmac, while the men stood behind and watched her go.

Bombfell elbowed Croom in the ribs. "This trip just became twice as intriguing!" Then he rushed to catch up to Nebula, trying not to spill what remained of his sherry.

"Yes...intriguing," Croom said, with only a fraction of Bombfell's enthusiasm.

❧

The plane engaged in a stellar take-off, sleek and speedy and without complication. Croom and Bombfell settled into their seats to continue their liquor-soaked discussion about how exactly the expedition would go, while Nebula familiarized herself with the region by reading several volumes on geography she'd thought to bring along from the museum's vast library.

"This tablet is surprisingly light for being so sizable," Croom pointed out as he examined it in greater detail. "How is that possible?"

"It's made of a substance called Featherstone," Bombfell explained. "There are sections of the Sarabezi that are rife with the stuff. It has another name in Zingali, of course. But every time I try to say it, I bite my tongue in three places."

Croom guffawed. "Their language sounds remarkable. I can't wait to sink my teeth into it."

"Alas, it's a dead language, Simeon. With no Zingaloo left to speak it, Twill's interpretation is the last mainstay for Zingali. But fear not—I'll teach you what I know of it! You'll be composing tongue-trill and spittle-thwit poetry in no time." The gentlemen clinked their glasses at the prospect.

"Because the world is just crying out for that," Nebula remarked, her eyes glued to the page of her geography book.

"Are you making any headway, Neb?" Croom asked. "Gaining a better sense of what might be in store for us when we finally reach our locale?"

Nebula ruffled the pages before her and looked even closer, as if her view of the actual terrain would somehow become clearer if only she could focus her vision a bit more. "Yes, I have actually...and it seems the passage along the Sarabezi River is nearly impenetrable, dense with practically impassible growth, if the maps and photos in these books are current."

"Oh, jungle flora," Bombfell lamented. "You shameless, selfish demon!"

Nebula paused and blinked at his ridiculous flair for the dramatic. "I suppose what I'm suggesting is that we'd be making the best use of our guide if we allowed him to determine our route through the surrounding jungle," she pointed out. "If he's knows the area as a native should, then perhaps he knows of a pass-through or a less-densely shrouded tract."

"A splendid idea!" Bombfell replied. "We should make certain to ask him as many questions as we can. And we should probably plan on writing down everything he says before he leaves, too."

"What do you mean, 'before he leaves'?" Nebula asked. She was coming to realize how tricky it could be communicating with this man, it was like speaking to a sphinx, if sphinxes had push-broom mustaches and pomade-slicked hairstyles.

"I mean that I might have...only been able...to secure him for one day," Bombfell said haltingly.

"And why would you ever secure a guide for only one day during what almost certainly promises to be a three-day excursion at the least?" Nebula asked, rightly unable to hide her concern.

"I've been told he's more than a little superstitious, and there are legends of mysterious supernatural creatures who dwell in the depths of the Sarabezi jungle," Bombfell explained. "The locals call them 'green men,' and according to lore, they appear out of nowhere to menace weary travelers, most of whom never return to tell the tale...and those who do are terrified to ever return again. A day's worth of travel will take us to the edge of where they're said to be, and thus he will go no further."

"Of course he won't," Nebula said with a fair amount of acid. She wondered why everything about this journey was precarious and difficult. Was it some sort of challenge Bombfell was presenting Croom—a proving of his loyalty, or his skill? Or was it their way to make things complicated on purpose, to heighten the sense of adventure that they both seemed so eager to recapture? It certainly appeared so far that they eschewed the spare and straightforward in favor of the complex and the corkscrewed. She could only hope that Croom was erring on the side of caution by allowing Bombfell to be responsible for any aspect of this endeavor, and that these mysterious arrangements would be far more amenable to their journey than she'd been led to believe. "Then we'll just have to make the most of our time with him, I suppose."

"We always do, don't we, Horatio?" Croom said.

Bombfell's attention was trained on Nebula, perhaps a bit too keenly. "I'm curious about something of a personal nature, Miss Everhope...I hope you don't think me rude."

"I do, but go on."

Bombfell couldn't help but appreciate her fire. "Did your gentleman understand when you told him you'd be gone for a week and a half, on an excursion with two dashing, rakish rogues such as Simeon and myself?" His question was forward and precisely composed, and accompanied by a lift of the eyebrows that lent an unwelcome weight, as if there were an extra question mark added to the end of his sentence though it clearly called for only one.

The whole suggestion flew like a dart into Nebula's craw.

Croom could see it in an instant. "You're making her uncomfortable, Horatio," he said protectively. "I won't allow it."

"I'm simply asking her a question," Bombfell said, his thumb flicking the rim of his glass as if prying at an unseen speck.

"Not that it's any of your business," Nebula answered, "but I'm not involved with anyone at the moment."

"Oh...I see," Bombfell said. It was loaded with suggestion. His eyes bobbed in Croom's direction.

"You see nothing but that overly-large nose at the end of your face, clouding your already-myopic vision," Croom said through a chuckle designed to dismiss the tension that kept slinking into the conversation. "Nebula and I are simply colleagues, co-conspirators in the effort to keep Hydewhite attractive and profitable, and nothing more."

"Is that true?" Bombfell's mustache wiggled mischievously.

"Absolutely," Nebula confirmed as she read.

Bombfell laughed like a carnival clown being tickled under the chin with a pickaxe. "Well, I can certainly understand your reticence to be involved in any other way with this scalawag, Miss Everhope. He was gangly and hunched in a corner at the back of the Mount Tumbledown library when I first found him, hiding away from modern civilization while he studied ancient ones with his nose buried in some high-minded literary work. He hardly knew how to speak to women then; it was a language he'd yet to master. And speaking to a *beautiful* woman in particular was a dialect so far out of his reach, I wasn't certain he'd ever become fluent."

Croom laughed with tremendous surprise. "Oh, I learned, Horatio. Believe me. I've spoken fluently to countless beautiful women over the years."

"And sometimes, they've even spoken back," Nebula said blandly.

Bombfell, with all his skill for secret intention and double meaning, easily detected a spot of curiosity in her witty remarks despite her flattened tone—a layer of protest in the crisp commentary with which she spoke to Croom in general that hinted at an interest beyond their professional relationship. He was certain it had never been expressed aloud. He said nothing of it, but cast his compatriot a challenging leer.

"My conquests are legendary!" Croom said, with too much confidence for someone who was telling the truth.

"Yes," Nebula said quietly, "if by 'legendary' you mean 'largely fictitious and highly exaggerated.'"

Croom choked on his lager.

"Well-played, Miss Everhope," Bombfell said with unsettling cheer. "The point goes to you!"

"Wonderful. Now, if we could focus on the details of this expedition rather than more seedy speculation regarding the romantic lives of anyone on this aircraft," Nebula insisted, "I'd feel much better about our chances of coming out of the Sarabezi with the object we're in search of—and with all of our limbs intact." She added *only one day with guide* and *green men* to the list of things they should be prepared for.

It seemed that list was growing by the minute.

"So this Heavencrest mountain range where Twill believed Thoiink embedded the Treasure Star," Croom began, his scientific deduction voice growing in volume, "it's a large area, I'd imagine, judging by its name?"

"Colossal," Bombfell agreed. "There are seventeen peaks that nearly encircle the Sarabezi like a jagged, verdant halo."

Nebula held up the geography book. "And according to these charts, the sacred volcano Bazoot is practically dead-center amid the mountains, which means the Treasure Star could be virtually anywhere among them."

"Dr. Twill was convinced that the tablet held some sort of secret that would lead him to the right location eventually," Bombfell said, "perhaps a message in the symbols that suggested a map of some sort, though he was never able to discern what they meant. He did make two trips to the region himself, though aside from bringing back the tablet, he returned from both empty-handed."

"If he travelled there himself, he must have kept a log or a journal of some sort," Croom prompted.

"Sadly, there was a great fire at his home after his death, during which his every possession was reduced to ashes, including the maps and charts from his excursions along the Sarabezi."

Nebula found this entirely too coincidental, perhaps even more than all the other coincidences thus far. "How unfortunate," was the only comment she made.

Bombfell stared at the floor mournfully. "Indeed."

"Well, I don't think it's in our best interest on this trip to climb mountain after mountain looking far and wide for a potentially fictitious item just to prove that your Dr. Twill wasn't incorrect in believing it exists, using a stone tablet that he *thought* might be helpful in finding it." Nebula knew this couldn't possibly have been Bombfell's plan, though it seemed more likely every minute.

Croom scratched his chin. "Actually, we've gone on more extensive excursions with lesser justification."

Bombfell clapped his hands loudly. "Remember the time when we—"

Nebula watched Croom's eyes come alive as he heard it and thought it best to shut down this new round of Remember the Time before they lost the rest of the day to old adventures instead of working out the remaining details of the new one. "We should at least gather an idea of which section of these mountains we're aiming for, don't you think?" she persisted. "Otherwise, we'll have no clue how to calculate our route, or how long our provisions will last...and our guide will be gone before the journey has truly begun. Even an educated guess will do at this point, since we have little else to go on." She seemed to be the only one in the vicinity too practical to possess even a slight sense of adventure.

But her practicality was proving to be even more of a necessity all the time.

"She's right, Horatio," Croom agreed. "We should make a plan."

Bombfell nodded enthusiastically. "Absolutely. Let's do just that."

"You mean, you had no other plan in mind?" Nebula asked. Both men shook their heads, so vigorously their hair nearly fell out of place.

"We tend to fly by the seat of our pants," Croom pointed out.

Nebula wondered how Bombfell thought they'd ever get anywhere with this endeavor when he'd come to Croom so unprepared. "Well, I don't."

"Another reason we're so lucky to have you onboard," Bombfell chimed.

Nebula's finger slid along the page as she tried to put their silliness aside. "We'd do best to begin from the eastern-most ridge and work our way north, then west," she postulated. "The passage looks far less dense."

Bombfell pressed his forefinger to his temple, as if it helped him focus his memory. "Yes—now that I think about it, I do believe that was how Dr. Twill described his excursions: traveling east to west."

Croom leaned over Nebula's shoulder and examined the map for himself. "But it looks like it might be easier to approach from the west and work our way eastward, doesn't it—like the slope of these peaks might be more accommodating, even with the thicker foliage?"

"Ah, yes - THAT was it," Bombfell affirmed, his memory finger now wagging in the air above his head. "He began in the west and worked his way east."

Nebula gazed and Bombfell with her lips wrinkled in perplexity. "Well, which was it, Dr. Bombfell? Surely you have some definite, unshifting remembrance of your conversations with Dr. Twill. He was your mentor, after all... wasn't he?"

Bombfell cast her a look unlike the others he'd given, one that gave her a glimpse of what lay behind his façade of high manners. "I do hope you'll forgive me, Miss Everhope. The grief over his death has made my mind go a bit foggy."

His tone chilled her, even if his sentiment was sincere.

Croom held the stone tablet and studied it for a moment, hoping to glean a clue that he'd somehow overlooked during earlier observation. It looked like a clay vessel that had somehow been sliced open down the back in a jagged, zigzagging seam and rolled out nearly flat, save for a bit of wiggle and warp, which made it terribly interesting overall but lent no insight regarding its usefulness. His finger ran along the outline of the six-pointed shape in the center that looked quite like a captain's wheel with an arrow and a triangle superimposed upon it. "What does this represent, Horatio—do you know?"

Bombfell glanced in Croom's direction without moving an inch closer. "Dr. Twill believed that was the symbol of the god Shtaaa, the bestower of the orb."

"Fascinating," Croom murmured. "I've never seen anything like it."

There were also the three symbols embossed in faint relief in the center: a disk, a cylinder, and an oval pinched to a point at each end, and beneath it all, a small round impression the size of a coin sat above a deep triangular groove. He ran his fingertip against each in succession as if they would release their secrets if grazed by his confident touch. They did nothing of the sort. "These symbols in and of themselves don't do us a scrap of good, do they?"

The tablet cast an irritating shadow on the book as Nebula read, the light from the overhead bulbs allowing pinholes of illumination to puncture the darkness. "Simeon, please; I can't see what I'm reading from the...shadow of...the tablet." Her eyes refocused on the spots of light that landed on the paper in front of her. "Well, heaven's glow..."

"No, Neb—Heaven's *Halo*," Croom corrected her. "You were close though."

"Actually, it's Heavencrest, old man!" Bombfell corrected him.

Nebula was too wrapped up in her new revelation to even hear them. "Hold the tablet higher, Simeon," she said, pushing his hands up and up, until he was holding the tablet over his head. The light made a scattering of little round sparks all over the geography book and the table it rested upon. "Dr. Twill was right; it *is* a map...but it isn't of the terrain." She flipped to the blank pages at the back of the book, then took a pencil and traced each spot of light onto the paper where it fell through the shadow of the tablet. "It's a map of the night sky."

Croom lowered the tablet to find a series of circles now drawn onto the paper. "Well, isn't that brilliant?" he said.

Nebula glanced at him sideways. "Do you mean the discovery, or the tablet itself?"

Croom chuckled. "Both, I believe."

"What would be truly brilliant is if I could figure out which constellation it is." She turned the book this way and that, then this way again, then halfway-that and half-way-this. "It doesn't look the slightest bit familiar to me."

"Remember: they worshiped the stars—all of them," Bombfell reminded her. "They had constellations of their own, entirely unrelated to those we know."

"Considering the visibility of the sky hasn't changed drastically in two thousand years, they'd have used the same stars overall. If I can identify anchoring patterns, I may be able to make some assumptions about the major stars, and how corresponding asterisms might overlap..." She was speaking aloud for their benefit, but it also proved purposeful to clarify her own thoughts. Still, it sounded ingenious of her, which wasn't the least bit surprising to Croom.

Bombfell seemed undeniably pleased with the development as well. "Impressive," he said creakily.

Nebula ignored everything but the page in front of her. "If my time in the Hydewhite planetarium serves me like it should, I'd say this..." and she pointed to a cluster of circles toward the edge of the book, "...is Hebridus the Blacksmith, and these..." and she pointed to a line of spots along the crease, "...would be the Double-Spined Daglir and their arching talons on either side, which would make these..." and she pointed to a V-shaped grouping that angled downward, "...the Sahira, the lovely sisters of the K4 galaxy."

"And all of this means...what, exactly?" Croom asked.

"If I had to guess—and we have no other option at this point—I'd say whoever created this map was illustrating the sky that hovers above the location of the Treasure Star. All we need to do is identify the mountain these constellations reside over, and the location of the relic should be revealed."

"Oh my," Bombfell said from the bottom of his throat, as if he were swallowing a spoonful of butterscotch. "She is a shrewd one, isn't she?"

Nebula's head whipped in Bombfell's direction. "She's also within earshot, and she doesn't like being referred to in third person."

"It was a grave mistake to make," Bombfell told her with false regret. "I meant no disrespect."

"Of course you did, Dr. Bombfell," Nebula disagreed. "It appears to be your basest instinct."

Croom may not have been an expert in astronomy, but he was aware of one celestial reality that might still have thrown them off-course just a touch. "Don't the locations of the stars vary during different times of the year, Neb?"

"They do, yes." Nebula took the tablet from Croom's hand and examined the symbols on its surface for herself once more. "But in conjunction with the star chart, these symbols have a different meaning. I would imagine the circle poised over the triangle indicates where the sun is in relation to the mountain at the time of year that the constellation is in place, like a sort of calendar to let the holder know when exactly the tablet would be most pertinent." She cast a suspicious eye at Bombfell as he poured himself yet another drink. "And I'd have to assume that we're in just the right time of year for all of this to be fully relevant to the Sarabezi region. Am I wrong, Dr. Bombfell?"

Bombfell looked as surprised as Croom did. "I certainly hope you aren't, Miss Everhope! We'd have gone all this way for nothing if that's true."

"Would we?" she asked pointedly.

As he was prone to doing, Bombfell appealed to his history with Croom to put things in perspective, skewed though it may have been. "To be honest, Simeon, I asked you on the journey not only for us to have another adventure together, but also because your crafty sensibilities and lithe mind have made such strange discoveries and accumulated so much obscure knowledge that I felt as if you'd be the only one with the skills necessary to make sense of this puzzle and find the Treasure Star."

"Horatio—you flatterer, you!" Croom basked in the glow of Bombfell's praise. Nebula was more than a little nauseated by it.

"But I must say now," Bombfell went on, "that Miss Everhope has put both your sensibilities and mine to shame. She's a mite smarter than either of us—maybe even cannier than Dr. Twill himself—and quite the asset to have along on a trip as fraught with mystery as this one."

"Oh," Croom said, somewhat disappointed by that, even though he felt entirely the same. "Well, yes...I thoroughly agree with your assessment. She's always been a steel-trap thinker."

Bombfell bowed his head in her direction. "Indisputably so."

Nebula's already clear-eyed vision for reading people had adapted during her short time with Bombfell; she was now acutely attuned to his adulation and could only see it as a device meant to cover the lack of contribution he was making to their journey. "Perhaps we could be finished complimenting one another and spend some time plotting our course into the Sarabezi before we leap out of an experimental plane and land knee-deep in a jungle none of us has ever been in before," Nebula suggested.

"Of course we can, Neb," Croom said brightly. "It would seem the next logical step."

"It certainly would, now that we have some idea of where we'll be headed," Bombfell concurred. "Though I'm sure there are still surprises a-plenty to be uncovered on this little adventure."

Of that possibility, Nebula had zero doubt.

FIVE

The foliage that surrounded the Sarabezi River was ridiculously dense and insidiously difficult to negotiate, even for a duo of explorers such as Simeon Croom and Horatio Bombfell, who had seen their fair share of rainforest terrain. It may have been simply the shimmering gleam of fond memory that altered their recollection, but it always seemed like this sort of landscape had cooperated with them in days past, pushing aside to the pressure of their boots and loosening at the force of their firm hands, as if to say, "Greetings, brave travelers, and a gracious good welcome to our part of the world—behold our wild wonders and revel in our rare and rustic beauty!" This time, it felt as if everything might be reaching out for them, pulling them back from their destination and choking off their path, with a message more along the lines of, "We laugh at your puny machete and your so-called courage. Best of luck to you, dimwits!"

As impressive as Nebula's map-reading skills were on the plane, they were doubly so in the field as she made certain that their trail was leading them in an advisable direction and not toward some vine-tangled dead-end or over an unforeseen cliff that only appeared to be solid ground all the way forward. None of this was easy when following the course of a river that seemed to zigzag in impossible ways every chance it got. It felt as if the Sarabezi were trying to shake them off the trail of the Treasure Star nearly as much as the oppressive foliage was.

"I haven't worked this hard in years," Croom sang out as he swung at the low-hanging branches with his machete.

"Neither have I," Bombfell said, though he didn't seem to do any work at all as he walked, always three paces behind as Croom cleared the path. He dabbed his brow with his handkerchief as if all the liquid in his body were being squeezed from him at once, and he took deep swigs from his canteen at frequent intervals to replenish it (though it contained gin instead of water), but he left all the vine-chopping and path-clearing to his more-than-able friend. "Watch those roots, old man—you nearly tripped and fell flat on your face!"

"So I did, Horatio!" Croom laughed. "So I did!"

Nebula walked between the two, listening to their bantering complaints as she considered the possibility that their penchant for adventuring might have been better off remaining in the distant past. She also wondered, with all of the blustery boom-and-blast Bombfell tossed about regarding how intrepid both he and Simeon were in their glory days, had he actually been of any help on their prior journeys at all ...or had he left all the difficult labor to Croom, much as he was doing now.

Bringing up the rear of their entire group rather than being in front as someone who was doing the job properly would have been was their guide, Orutal. He was a stout, sturdy man from a neighboring village settlement, and his English was as broken as a window pane trampled by elephants and fed through a laundry wringer. He knew only enough odd phrases for less-than-helpful assistance when asked, though he never offered it freely, and it always came with strange hand gestures, as if he were purposely trying to confuse them, too. "This for the go-go, away—AWAY!" was a common one; it came with a finger aimed straight down that instilled no confidence. "Water seeing? Here-here-here," was another; that one was accompanied by a double hand-swivel, as though he were trying to shake off sock puppets from both hands. Though he understood it no better than anyone else, Croom's favorite of all turned out to be, "Help in the happy times, but tasty? Per*haaaaaps*." It came with three fingers held aloft.

Ortual seemed to be the only one who knew what any of it meant.

There were the added limitations that he was unbelievably myopic and wore spectacles that were essentially magnifying glasses held together with rusted wire; that he required occasional naps nestled in the broad arms of the Waliki trees to keep his energy level up; and that he walked slowly and with a limp, the result of a tussle with a jaguar that had somehow found its way into his family's hut one night and was raiding their peanut butter supply. All of this was explained by Bombfell as last-minute complications to an already-challenging situation. And in spite of his status as a native to the area, Orutal seemed to have no devotion whatsoever to the Zingaloo mythology that these three sought so fervently. He could lend nothing to their search from that standpoint. "Lost people, lost stories," he said of them, which made a surprising amount of sense given their mysterious history. But he followed it up with, "I shall save my money and buy a monkey instead!" which, once again, made no sense whatsoever. It did, however, cause the crew to question where he'd come into contact with anyone who would have spoken English in this manner.

Currently, Orutal was yodeling folk songs in his native tongue and snacking on large green berries that he continuously plucked out of the trees as if he were pulling treats from a holiday stocking. "And how did you come upon this so-called guide?" Nebula asked as they walked, once it became apparent that he would be of even less assistance than Bombfell.

"A friend of a friend of an acquaintance made the recommendation," Bombfell told her, "based on something overheard on a radio station during a bus trip."

That sounded very Bombfellian. "So a trusted source, then, is what you're telling us," she said sharply. "Well done."

Bombfell smirked. "Trust is a currency we spend sparingly when in the depths of adventure, Miss Everhope."

Nebula's brow creased. "It certainly seems that way, Dr. Bombfell."

"Luckily, we have you to stand in his stead, Neb," Croom called out. "Your study of those maps has really paid off! And you've remained so composed the whole time. While we're sweating away like dock workers running a marathon on a late-July afternoon, you've hardly even gathered a sheen."

Bombfell dabbed his forehead again. "Yes...you have a remarkable composition."

"And our more massive forms practically battle as we slice our way through a dense forest network that you negotiate by slipping your lithe shape in the spaces between," Croom noted, "as if stepping through the gaps in a spider web without touching the strands on either side. You seem nearly as versed in tromping through the undiscovered as we are. If I didn't know better, I'd say you'd been on something of an adventure at some point yourself...maybe even a few."

"And you might indeed know better, Simeon," Nebula replied, "if you'd ever stop boasting incessantly about your own achievements long enough to ask me about mine." She was breathing quite regularly while the two men continued to huff and chug. It seemed that pushing through a living ecosystem required quite a different level of physical fitness than did performing acrobatic bar tricks. Nebula had just the right amount of whatever it took.

"I wouldn't say I boast *incessantly* about them," Croom protested.

Nebula let out a musical laugh that ended with a rappling snort. "Well, you haven't stopped since I reported to your office on my first day at Hydewhite. That seems pretty incessant to me."

They had come quite suddenly to a clearing that bathed them in sticky sunlight and revealed a three-pronged fork in the path, as though the jungle was waggling its serpent tongue and taunting them to push onward only if they dared. Croom came slashing through behind her, with Bombfell following carefully at his heels, while Orutal took his sweet, berry-stained time catching up to the three travelers he was supposed to be leading.

"Bumblestuff!" Croom exclaimed. "A riddle has reared its triple-headed confusion right in the midst of our conundrum."

"Three directions to lead us on, but only one that leads us toward our glorious destiny in the skies of the ancients," Bombfell intoned as he stroked his mustache.

"For someone putting forth so little effort, you certainly make this relic sound significant, Dr. Bombfell," Nebula pointed out.

"We wouldn't be here if it weren't, Miss Everhope," Bombfell struck back, sounding as if Nebula's overly-perceptive charm was beginning to wear on his nerves.

"What does Orutal have to say about it?" Croom inquired.

Their guide was as perplexed by the split road as they were, but the berries had been sweet, and the sugar made him smile his way through it. "Which way should you go?" he asked merrily, with unexpectedly well-intentioned ignorance.

"Shouldn't we be asking *you* that question?" Croom inquired.

Orutal shrugged and laughed. "I haven't saved enough to buy my monkey yet." It was as logical as anything else he'd said.

"Perhaps we should take a little time to reassess our position and better determine which mountain we're headed toward," Nebula suggested. She drew the book of maps from her pack and opened it on the ground before them. Her shadow fell like a silken silhouette upon the paper, shading her vision from the sharp glare of the overhead sun well enough to read the print. She followed with her finger the path they'd taken thus far, until she found what appeared to be the small pitchfork split in the trees. "If we presume ourselves to be located here, then the peaks lie ahead beyond the thickening jungle there." She glanced ahead of them, to a spot where the foliage redoubled itself and shared not even a hint of the secret places that might lie yonder. Then she pointed to the left, her finger finding a Waliki tree as broad and wide as any in the vicinity. "Our only hope is to climb this tree and see what the horizon tells us."

"Perfect deduction, Neb!" Croom exclaimed.

"Perhaps we should ask Orutal to do the legwork on this one," Bombfell suggested as they moved toward the tree. "He should do more to earn his wage than just gorging himself and slowing us down with his naps." But when they turned to make the request, they found no sign of their failure of a guide, other than a small pile of green berry skins stacked up in the shape of a little human figure.

"Where'd he go?" Nebula asked, her neck craning as she searched for evidence of his departure behind them.

"Maybe his stomach became upset from eating so many berries," Croom proposed. "We've found ourselves in similar gastronomical situations many a time on the road, eh, Horatio?"

"I fear it's something quite different, actually," Bombfell commented as he scrutinized the berry-skin sculpture. "I believe we've entered the territory of the green men. And this is his warning to us about them, as much as his farewell."

At once, the berry skins took on a far more sinister significance.

"Let's keep our eyes and ears open at all times, folks," Croom implored them. "We don't need any casualties this far into the game." He turned sharply and stumbled on a boulder that was far too large to have been missed. "Whoops. I suppose that includes me, too."

Nebula sighed.

"You're an expert climber, Horatio," Croom reminded him as he stood again and brushed his hands clean. "Why don't you scramble up the tree and see what's what?"

"You know how much I would love to do just that, Simeon," Bombfell hemmed and hawed, "but you see, I fear all the walking we've done so far has taken a toll on my fallen arches."

"You can cartwheel and somersault for hours at Murphy's, but you can't climb a simple tree?" Croom asked. "That isn't like you."

"I'm as surprised by it as anyone," Bombfell said morosely. "I'm not certain I'll have the strength to finish the trek, even, let alone scurry into the high branches of a Waliki."

Nebula had come to expect no less from him. "I'll go, then," she said firmly, stretching her shoulders and loosening up her neck. "It's been ages since I climbed a tree, and I don't often get the chance anymore being locked up at the museum all day long like I am."

"No, Neb," Croom said with an authoritative shake of his head. "I'll go. I've played surveyor many times over in my life. My visual acuity hasn't been put to proper use this entire trip, and I should do something to make up for the whole navigational oversight. You wouldn't even be here with us at all if not for that. And I won't have you risk your safety for us if my safety can be risked instead." Croom had often employed this sort of chivalry when he was out entertaining a woman, but it usually pertained to taking the seat near the aisle at the cinema in hopes of sparing his date from popcorn spills and soda splashes delivered at the hands of clumsy oafs who weren't careful enough to watch where they were going in darkened theaters. It was generally an overwhelming success, and won him the adoration of many a young lady who fell for simple and obvious gallantry.

But the Sarabezi jungle was no cinema, and Nebula Everhope wasn't one of his adoring crowd.

"I'll have you know, Simeon, that I have scaled more trees in more uncharted areas of the world than you've likely ever seen. I've swung from the limbs of the Ubotso trees in the Lower Crigg Basin in search of moon fruit when my company had entirely run out of rations, and I've aped about in Banutu trees at the Gardens of Yedain while evading savage hordes of parrot bats that weren't willing to listen to reason, and I've bedded down in hammocks tied between the arms of the holy Haka-Haka trees on the Shidara Peninsula—twenty feet off the ground, no less...and I've never even come close to falling out." She folded her arms and stood staunch and tall, emulating the very tree behind him that she intended to climb, even if she had to scramble over him first to get to it. "And on and on and on I could go, if you'd like me to."

"I, um...wow." Croom was thunderstruck, as much by her emphatic protest as by her previously unshared secret life as an international tree climber.

"Well now, Miss Everhope," Bombfell said, his diction crisp, his tone accusatory. "You have stories to share, haven't you?"

"Yes, Neb...what else haven't you been telling us?" Croom asked, his suspicious eyebrow bent like a boomerang. "Me in particular."

It was more than Simeon Croom's boasting that had kept Nebula from exposing the truth about herself. It was her reluctance to be considered based on the merits of who she was related to rather than who she was and what she was capable of. But she knew she'd said too much now to not explain herself, at least in some small manner. "I spent the better part of my childhood traveling with my father around the globe in search of medicinal herbs to treat and eradicate various infectious diseases. It took us to practically every corner of the planet, and it exposed me to learning opportunities I wouldn't have known otherwise, just perfect for a child with an immense curiosity and eyes that could hardly open wide enough to take in the whole world around her."

"That wasn't on your resume," Croom pointed out.

"No...it wasn't," Nebula said. "But his work was very important, and the experience I garnered while traveling with him comes in handy at moments like these, when maps and stone tablets can only take us so far, and trees need climbing, and terrain needs surveying to continue the journey." That was all she intended to say about the matter, at least in front of Horatio Bombfell. "Now, if you wouldn't mind stepping aside, I'll take a quick shuffle up this beast of a tree, and we can be on our way."

Croom's gaze lingered a bit too long on Nebula's insistent eyes, on her determined chin and her unwavering, confident posture before he realized she was issuing a command. "Oh, yes. Yes of course." He stepped away and bowed at the waist, his extended arm sweeping her forward as if she were royalty. "Your tower awaits."

"Spare me the condescension, Simeon. I've had more than my fill on this trip already." Then she planted her right boot squarely on the knobby root of the tree, reached high for a handhold on a gnarled section just above her, and scurried into the tree top high overhead.

She was gone from their vision in three blinks.

Nebula pushed through the canopy and found the lay of the land to be far more chaotic than she'd expected from viewing the map; it seemed that the Sarabezi jungle had experienced some sort of growth explosion, with new foliage covering everything in sight like luxuriant emerald fur. Fortunately, the peaks stood prominently above it all. Bazoot could be seen in the near-distance as a center-point, lazily exhaling vapor as if he was someone's rich uncle smoking a cigar. But the revelation of which region of Heavencrest they should be headed for was made no more obvious up there than it had been from down be-low...that was, until Nebula noticed something peculiar about the shape those mountains took on when viewed as a unit rather than one peak at a time.

"Simeon!" she called down at the top of her voice. "I need the tablet...I think I've found something terribly significant!"

Croom and Bombfell shared a look of incredulous excitement, one they'd exchanged on many occasions. Then Croom gathered the tablet from his pack and scuttled up the tree himself, with Bombfell watching from below.

"Here it is, Neb!" Croom said, his arm extended high with the tablet in hand before his head was visible above the canopy.

Nebula snatched the tablet from him and held it out, sliding it back and forth, and from side to side, then turning it upside-down and flipping front-to-back, until she was finally able to make the jagged zigzag seam line up with the peaks on the horizon. "It's more than just a map of the stars above...it's a template of the landscape as well."

"So the tablet can be used to locate the proper peak by starlight at night if necessary," Croom surmised as he tilted his head to see the tablet overlaid against the horizon, "or by the shape of the mountains in the daylight instead."

"And if we follow those two pieces of logic to the assumption they make," Nebula continued, "then the

"*The rocks are, too...*"

"Only *certain* rocks, Horatio," Croom countered. "If geology taught us nothing else, it taught us that—"

"Rocks aren't alive, Simeon," Nebula said as she hopped out of the tree and landed squarely between the two men. "Geology has taught you nothing."

"Are you sure?" Croom asked.

"Yes, I am, and so is everyone else in any field of science, as well as grade schoolers, high schoolers, middle schoolers, infants, toddlers, the middle-aged, the elderly, and the entire rest of humanity. Rocks are not ali—" Nebula's protest was cut short by the sight of the boulder behind Croom rising up to the full height of him, then rising even taller...then sprouting arms and eyes. She pointed at the abomination growing in their midst. "Holy stratified drift—it *is* alive!"

Croom turned to find the boulder that he'd nearly tripped over earlier now outsized him by a factor of two. It had also developed eyes and was staring absolute hellfire in his direction. Somehow, he was unfazed by the strange implausibility of it all, though his colleagues had grown more than terrified.

Croom smiled smugly. "I told you so." It was mere seconds before the trees on either side of them shuffled into motion, and just a few seconds further before the unlikely living boulder raised its arm and delivered Croom a solid blow to the back of his head.

He fell unconscious at the roots of the Waliki tree, smashing the little green berry-skin man flat as he landed.

SIX

"Egads," Bombfell said in a hush. "This is simply astonishing!"

Nebula was far too concerned with what had just happened to Croom to be dazzled by any of it. "Simeon!" she cried out as she fell to his side. "Are you all right?"

Croom eased up on his elbows and shook his head as though the pain in it would just fly away at some point. "Did that rock just hit me on the back of the head with... itself?"

Nebula offered no dispute. "It does appear that way."

The adventurers turned to face the jungle as it came to life in a manner which none of them could ever have anticipated. It was as if the landscape was now a living jigsaw, breaking apart and falling out of its frame, with pieces sliding forward in the texture and pattern of the trees, the greenery, the stones—even the sky—and every single one in the unmistakable shape and size of a full-grown man. The entire jungle rearranged itself, its elements stepping forward and making themselves known as things entirely detached from their surroundings.

"The green men are no mere superstition," Bombfell gasped as the implication of such a thing hit him squarely in his push-broom mustache. "They're as real as Sarabezi itself." His eyes were wide and shining with dark wonder.

Croom's swimming, throbbing head found just as much amazement in it all as Bombfell did. "And they've evolved camouflaging capabilities to blend in with their environment in a near-perfect manner, rendering them practically invisible. Just look at the adaptive patterning on their skin...how unexpected!"

Nebula leaned forward carefully with her hands raised, doing her best not to anger these men whose limbs seemed to have evolved into weapons of various shapes and sizes as well, mostly spears and stone clubs and curved blades that looked like crescent moons with edges honed sharp for ready slicing. Then she realized she was actually adhering to the logic of Simeon Croom, which sometimes had crimps and kinks in it that made other possibilities seem far preferable. "That isn't evolution, Simeon. It's a disguise. They've dressed themselves in leaves and tree bark and stone and coated their skin with paints made of cla—OH!"

The man reached for Nebula's hand and pulled her toward him, spinning her around and clutching her neck in the crook of his elbow.

"Unhand her!" Croom called out, leaning against the Waliki trunk as he struggled back to his feet. His head swooned, and his sodden vision wasn't helping matters. Still, he raised his fists like a boxer readying for round one, prepared to swing full-force at all of them if necessary, and the other men raised their weapons against Croom and Bombfell as if to warn them away from attempting to rescue her. Then Croom made a stumbling leap toward them, for which he was rewarded with another smack on the back of the head, though this one came from the end of a spear. It was much gentler than being clubbed with a stone, but it sent him back to the ground on his hands and knees nonetheless.

The green men issued a strange hooting noise at the ridiculous interloper who couldn't seem to keep himself upright, no matter how hard he tried.

Nebula winced and gave a disappointed wheeze, though her captor's hold made it quite difficult. "Not to worry, Simeon. The situation is under control, as always." While the tribe was distracted by Croom's unintentionally amusing clumsiness, she took advantage of the distraction and swung her elbow back into her captor's ribcage. Then, while he was bent over her trying to gather his wind, she gripped his arm with both hands and spun him over her shoulder, landing him flat on his back on the jungle floor next to Croom.

The green men fell silent.

They came alive in a second, shaking their weapons wildly and crying out in shrill, whooping shrieks. They helped up their dazed and fallen tribesman and pushing Bombfell into the center next to Nebula as Croom scrambled groggily to his feet. Then they fell eerily silent, all at once, as if they were controlled by a single source, and the entire troupe turned and began walking back in the direction from which they'd just come, with the captives being pushed along in the center of them.

"I don't think they were as impressed with your display as we were, Neb," Croom said over the din. "It was quite a demonstration, though. Well delivered!"

"Yes—a right good show, Miss Everhope," Bombfell said sarcastically as he reared back from a swinging branch that missed his cheek by a whisper. "You've gotten yourself out of a small scrape by getting us into an entirely larger one."

"As if we've never been surrounded by screeching, hostile tribesmen before, Horatio," Croom reminded him, swiveling away from a prodding club aimed at his kidneys. "It's all part of the adventure."

"I think we've had as much adventure as we can handle for the moment," Nebula said as she dodged a poke in the shoulder from one of the spears. Then she tapped one of the green men on the arm, the one in front of her who seemed to be the leader. He wore a tall headdress of rubber tree leaves, which made it look like he had a potted plant on his head, and a mask made of bark, which didn't help matters. She took him to be their chief, and hoped to make her feelings known to him and his entire tribe, before one of their weapons sliced off an appendage or ruptured an organ; these three may have been intrepid adventurers, but they were still only soft-handed Westerners who punctured easily and bled profusely.

The chief paid her no attention.

"Listen here, sir," she said loudly yet firmly as she walked. "We have just as much right to be wandering about in your jungle as you have. Sure, we may not have been certain of where we were going before, but we're clear about it now. You have no cause to treat us this way, and I insist that you release us at once."

The chief said nothing, though he did roll his eyes rather openly.

Croom laughed a bit. "Is this how your father taught you to speak to natives when you stumble upon them in high disguise while you're potentially desecrating their sacred homes, and they take you captive with weapons that could easily remove your head in a blink?"

"No," Nebula told him. "We never encountered natives. I'm improvising."

"Clearly," Croom replied.

"It's a fat lot better than what you two are doing, Simeon. Which would be...what, again?"

Croom's forehead rumpled like a wad of giftwrap. "Surviving by holding my tongue, mostly. It's served me quite well in the past. I have great faith that it will do the same for me now."

Finally, the leader of the green men turned roughly, stopped the processional, and leaned into the faces of the three adventurers. *"Pop-pop-clickety-click-click-thwip-clack-doink! Doink! Dooooooooink!"*

Bombfell gasped. "Great Sickle of Grood!"

Croom was strangely intrigued and, in an odd and unexpected way, relieved to recognize the pattern of sounds coming from the chief's rapidly-flapping mouth. "Is that...?"

"It is!" Bombfell said. "They speak Zingali—the language of the Zingaloo survives!"

Even Nebula couldn't help being a tad excited by it. "So what did he say?"

Bombfell's muzzle drew down as he worked out the translation in his head, mostly by dancing his eyebrows all about his forehead. "I believe he said, 'You people are louder...than a waterfall filled with hiccupping chimpanzees.'"

"Are you sure that's what it was?" Croom asked.

It wasn't as if Bombfell had expected to hear an extinct language being spoken by a tribe of men who were largely considered to be a folktale, so he hadn't listened as closely as he might have otherwise. "As I told you, Simeon, I'm far from fluent," he answered. "But his comment would certainly be justified. We haven't stopped chattering since they captured us."

"Say something back to them!" Croom encouraged him. "Tell them we come in peace, and we hope we haven't offended them by us coming unannounced to their lovely yet treacherous jungle!"

"They're holding us at spear-point, and it's quite likely they've just compared us to chimpanzees," Nebula reminded him. "I think it's safe to say they're a mite offended."

Bombfell did his best to offer their apology. *"Click-click-thwiiiiip-thwip-thwip-pop-POPpop."*

The green men looked at one another uneasily, as if each hoped the others around him would understand what their poorly-spoken invader had said.

"Poppop-pop doink click-clock-cloooook-thwip-pbbbbbtttt," said the chief in return.

Bombfell nodded like a bolt had come loose in his neck and the spring that held his head in place was free to do as it pleased. "Ah, yes, yes...I suppose."

"What did he say?" Nebula asked.

"Yes, tell us!" Croom added.

"He said I speak Zingali worse than his toothless great-grandmother who lost half of her tongue in a diving accident." Bombfell blushed.

Nebula grimaced in a way that everyone around her was becoming accustomed to by now. "How helpful."

"Perhaps you could tell them about the Treasure Star," Croom suggested, "since it is the only reason we've invaded their terrain at all."

"That's what I was trying to do," Bombfell admitted. "I'm afraid they were unable to understand me. Should I try again, only louder and slower this time?"

Before Croom had a chance to suggest that they had nothing to lose for it, Nebula reached for Croom's waistband to retrieve the tablet. "Pardon my touch, Simeon," she said matter-of-factly.

"Erm, not at all, Neb," Croom said, doing his best not to giggle as her frisky fingers brushed a particularly ticklish section of his back.

Nebula handed Bombfell the tablet. "Show him this. I'm sure it speaks Zingali a thousand times better than you."

"Sprightly thinking, Miss Everhope, if I do say so," Bombfell said as he held the tablet before him.

First, the chief's face drew down toward the table and eyelids squeezed together to scrutinize it. Then they widened all the way, and his mouth fell open, his teeth shining brilliantly through his bark mask, as if the tree he pretended to be had sprout an entire face before their very eyes.

"I think he recognizes it!" Bombfell cried.

"*Click-click-cliiiiiiiick!*" the chief said, turning to his troops, and then repeated himself, "*Click-click-cliiiiiiiick!*"

Then the entire tribe of green men slowly lowered their spears and clubs and branches and took up the same *click-click-cliiiiiiiick* chant that the chief made. They sounded it out over and over again as the whole lot of them ever so gradually fell to their knees and bowed their heads until their noses touched the rich jungle soil.

"Is this a good thing, do you suppose?" Nebula asked.

"None of us have spears in our chests or stone clubs embedded in our skulls," Croom pointed out as he turned carefully to survey the full circle of prostrated tribesmen, "and our heads are still attached to our bodies, so I'm inclined to say it isn't bad."

When the tribe stood again, their demeanor was entirely the opposite of what it had been before their chief relayed his message. They clapped Croom and Bombfell on the shoulders like they were meeting old friends for a drink at the pub, and they kissed Nebula's hands as if she were royalty arriving for a diplomatic visit.

"I think they're happy that we returned their tablet," Croom told her.

"*Click-clock-thwip-thwipthwip!*" the tribe said.

"I believe they're saying your beauty is like a mountain cleared of mud by a heavy rain," Bombfell told her.

"That's only slightly better than the hiccupping chimpanzee comment," Nebula said.

Croom took the tablet from Bombfell and addressed the chief himself for the first time, pointing first to the jagged edge, then to the horizon behind them through the jungle trees, toward the region of Heavencrest they'd identified as the location of the Treasure Star.

"Be careful if you attempt speaking to them," Bombfell said, with far more authority than someone who'd just botched a Zingali conversation should have. "Speaking their language is like walking a maze with your tongue... you might accidentally insist that they chop off our toes, or worse."

"*Clack-click-cloooooock-clock glug-glug-gulp-gulp-gulp thwip-thwip shhhlup doink-doink pop-pop-pop,*" Croom said, with an accent so polished and precise that, had he been wearing a grass kilt and a wreath of Waliki leaves on his head, he could have passed for one of the tribe.

The chief answered him in far more *clicks* and *pops* and *doinks* than those listening would have thought possible in a single breath. But it was a plausible answer, and it spoke volumes about Croom's facility with linguistics. Then the entire crowd burst into a much friendlier laughter, a sound that resembled bubbles popping in a bathtub filled with pancake syrup.

"Did you really just speak perfect Zingali after hearing only a smattering, Simeon?" Nebula asked. "Enough for him to offer you a lucid response?"

"I believe I did," Croom said, confidently. "Once you recognize the dipthongs and capture the syntax, the rest of it comes pretty easily."

"Instantaneous fluency," Bombfell said with tremendous admiration. "The man is truly awe-inspiring."

"Then he should *definitely* pick up French next," Nebula chided, if only to balance out the excessive admiration.

"What did you say to him?" Bombfell asked excitedly.

"I simply told him that we'd been given the tablet in hopes of finding the Treasure Star and inquired whether he knew the easiest way for us to get to the base," Croom told them. "And he replied that not only does he know the quickest and safest path to the mountain peak in question, but that his tribe will be more than happy to facilitate the journey to make certain we arrive safely, and that we return in one piece—or three pieces, as the headcount indicates."

"And why are they so willing to help us?" Bombfell asked.

"Yes, Simeon...why is that?" Nebula asked right behind him. "You didn't happen to promise them things you can't deliver, as you tend to do with the Hydewhite board of trustees, did you?"

"Not this time, Neb. They're willing to help because these highly-evolved—er, cleverly-disguised natives aren't simply the so-called green men, as the folklore would have us believe." Croom turned to his companions with as much dramatic flair and showmanship as he could muster on such short notice. "These, my friends, are members of what remains of the Zingaloo tribe...two thousand years after their rumored extinction."

That made even less sense to Nebula than the rest of the strangeness unfolding before them. "Then why would they ever allow us to search for a prized artifact from their distant past?"

Croom pulled at his collar and cleared his throat awkwardly. "Because the tribe as they are today no longer worships Shtaaa or any of the old gods; they don't believe there even is a Treasure Star to be found...and even if it had been a thing, the myth says that the orb was returned to the gods, which means it was taken into the sky, not up to a mountain top. Thoiink's myth is now nothing more than a bedtime story they tell their children to warn them of the dangers of wandering into the jungle at night."

"He said that?" Nebula asked.

"Yes. He thinks we're fools for trying."

"There could be an ancient relic tied to his own tribe's mythology resting on a mountain top in his midst, and he thinks we're fools for wanting to retrieve it?" Bombfell said. "He can't be serious."

Croom shrugged. "That last phrase he spoke most closely translates in English to, 'Best of luck, suckers; you'll be lucky if the snakes don't swallow you whole.'" He said it again in Zingali, and nodded to the chief to ascertain that he'd gotten it right. The chief nodded and smiled in return, the rubber tree fronds on his headdress bouncing emphatically.

Then the Zingaloo tribe erupted in syrupy, bubbling laughter once again.

SEVEN

Now that they had real guides to escort them through the Sarabezi jungle, the three adventurers shifted passage and walked where the Zingaloo led them, and although they had considered themselves the captives of the tribe just a short time earlier, Croom and Bombfell seemed entirely comfortable with this new development. Nebula, however, was still incredibly suspicious about what lay ahead for them. After all, there was a mountain to scale and an artifact to locate—if it existed at all; she knew that evidence pointing toward the existence of the Treasure Star was not the relic itself. Even with the chief's offer for his tribe to assist in what he believed was nothing more than a fool's errand, there was no guarantee that they'd have an easy time of it from here on out.

She also felt incredibly excluded being the only soul in the entire troupe who could neither speak nor understand even a few words in Zingali, and it irked her considerably.

In addition to everything else, they'd been taken so far astray from their original path by now that none of them had noticed what direction they were moving in, which effectively kept them from knowing where they were at the moment. The light that filtered down through the canopy was quickly dwindling, and soon there would be no sky above them by which to locate anything. Nebula knew that keeping some semblance of knowledge regarding their whereabouts at every moment was pivotal, especially having no idea where the Zingaloo were actually leading them. She now had to trust that Croom and his reptilian friend Bombfell had made the right decision in allowing this change of course, and that they wouldn't be savaged by whatever animals were growling and mewling and purring in the underbrush.

And there seemed to be quite a lot of that at the moment.

"I thought they were taking us to the mountains," Nebula said uneasily.

"That's for tomorrow," Croom informed her. "Right now, they're taking us to their village. We're to be their dinner guests."

"Meaning we'll join them for dinner rather than becoming their dinner, correct?" she asked cautiously.

Croom tsked. "They're natives, Neb. Not cannibals."

"You don't know that for certain...and might I point out that they were extinct until they leapt out of the jungle, knocked you on the head, and put me in a chokehold?" she reminded him. "The possibilities are endless."

"I think if they were going to eat us, they'd have us tied to poles rather than letting us walking alongside them like old friends, don't you?" Croom postulated.

Nebula leered at the tribesmen. "Things could turn at any moment."

Croom shook his head and began a boisterous conversation with the tribesmen, telling them witty tales in their own language about his former exploits tromping about the world. The Zingaloo laughed in the endearing bubble-popping way that they had, and every so often, Bombfell tried to contribute to the conversation by making comments in Zingali that translated to, "I believe there's a parrot in my shoe; if you'd be so kind as to bring me my toothbrush, I'll dig a hole in that tree trunk to set it free," or "It's not how many rocks you can hold in your underpants at one time that counts; it's how many you have left when you finally stop running," or "Bananas aren't the miracle food of the century, but you won't find a more delicious ashtray anywhere." Croom smoothed over the awkward, confused silences that ensued by explaining that his friend had been suffering from an unexpected bout of Roqan fever during the trip, and that his language skills had been compromised because of it. It wasn't true, of course, but the tribesmen rubbed Bombfell's arm with great sympathy every time.

"You seem to be winning them over as much as I am, Simeon," Bombfell said, having no idea what was really happening.

"We are quite the set of charmers, aren't we, Horatio?" Croom said back, hoping not to crush his comrade's spirit with the cumbersome weight of the truth.

Bombfell's laughter was thick and oblivious. "We've lost but a scrap of our old charisma over the years!"

Nebula wondered to herself how little Bombfell must have had to begin with to end up with what he had now, if all he'd lost was a scrap.

For all the toil and peril and mystery that still lay ahead of them on this adventure, Croom realized that he was absolutely having the time of his life. He wasn't certain now if he'd ever be able to do without experiences like this one once the excursion came to a close.

There was an unexpected shift in the foliage as they walked, as if someone had opened a florist shop in the middle of the jungle and gathered an unimaginable bounty of brilliantly-colored blooms with which to fill it. Some of them were so vivid they seemed to generate their own light. There were too many hues for Nebula's liking; she much preferred the shades of things that existed in a city environment, like stone, or concrete, or tweed. Even in her childhood, her own travels hadn't exposed her to so much raw color in one place.

"It's beautiful!" Croom said blithely. "Like an enormous birthday cake has sprung up right in the heart of the jungle!"

"Of course you would think that," Nebula replied. "Your socks are usually two different colors."

"Come on, Neb," Croom implored her. "Enjoy the scenery. The Zingaloo have turned out to be a friendly lot of chaps, and they've taken us into their care. Thanks to your superior deductive reasoning and your amazing capabilities with maps and astronomy, we have an incredibly focused idea of where to find the Treasure Star, even if they don't believe it's there. Our expedition is working out swimmingly."

"And so?" Nebula asked, as if she couldn't perceive his reasoning.

Croom laughed at her. "*And so* lighten up a bit!"

Nebula was letting his sentiment sink in when Bombfell dropped back and joined her. "Yes, Miss Everhope... lighten up, please. You're spoiling all the adventure in this adventure."

The mere sound of his voice made her spine sizzle now.

Just beyond this horticultural firework display was the reason for the sudden floral explosion: the Zingaloo had taken the explorers to their home along the banks of the Sarabezi River, with its vital waters as blue as a ribbon of sky rushing along at a rhythmic yet relaxing pace. Small rapids lay yonder, chuckling at the sliver of horizon showing in strips and swatches through the thick foliage. "Can you hear that?" Croom asked excitedly as they approached it.

"It's the river, yes," Nebula said. "It's about all I can hear at the moment."

"But listen closer to the sounds it makes." Croom stopped and focused, so Nebula did the same. "Their language isn't derived from spitting out bugs and feathers. The river has been the center of their lives for millennia...Zingali emulates all the sounds of water, not just the cheek-flicking doink."

Nebula listened again, and suddenly heard what Croom was suggesting. "Interesting," she admitted.

Croom now knew the chief with the rubber tree headdress by his Zingali name, Towhiit, which was pronounced with an incredibly entertaining little whistling noise at the end. Towhiit motioned for them to come forward. So Croom pushed through the ferns that hung like delicate fringed draperies from the limbs of the trees and the adventurers stepped into the Zingaloo village as it now existed: a surprisingly sleek collection of ladder-connected caverns built into the side of a cliff wall grown over with blossoming vines. A pillar embossed with cryptic symbols and pictograms stood in the center like statuary in a courtyard, with a ring of fire flickering brightly around the bottom and a circle of glowing torches stationed along the circumference to lend light. For being the jungle dwelling home camp of a tribal culture presumed to be extinct for two thousand years, it was astoundingly well-executed and well-preserved.

"They're tucked away in a nook where they could live forever if need be," Bombfell said, "which is apparently just what they've done—out of harm's way, out of sight of their fellow countrymen who simply presumed they'd disappeared, and sustaining their tribal ways for all this time. Their powers of survival are mind-boggling."

"Not so much when you think about how they've been hiding away in the jungle," Nebula said. "Practically anything can survive if concealed well enough." She seemed resistant to everything Bombfell suggested.

"Horatio is right, Neb," Croom told her. "It's a most significant discovery—like finding an extra cherry jelly bean at the bottom of the jar, tucked beneath all the licorice ones you've avoided eating."

"Is that your scientific assessment, Simeon?" Nebula asked.

"No," Croom said, slightly annoyed by her lack of awe. "It's my human one. You seem to have forgotten what it's like to have an adventure such as this, Nebula Everhope."

"I remember," she said. "Better than you think."

"Just look, then," he insisted. "Just listen."

Though she wasn't prone to indulging her senses when there was so much left to accomplish in such a short time, she did as he asked, watching, breathing in the perfume of the blooms, listening to the rush of the river that seemed to speak in the tongue of the Zingaloo. "It's...very special, isn't it?" she asked, allowing a bit of the Sarabezi magic to infiltrate her stoic facade. Finally, Nebula allowed herself to smile, though it was practically imperceptible.

Croom saw it, though.

"Yes; it is," he confirmed, with a much larger smile in return.

"There are wonders in this world beyond your wildest imagining, Miss Everhope," Bombfell said, with not nearly as much cheer as Croom had. His eyes narrowed to slits of extreme gravity as he spoke in her direction. "You'd do well to bear that in mind as this exploration proceeds."

Nebula wondered how Croom could be so unaware of the slithering tongue Bombfell used when speaking to her since they'd entered the jungle. It felt as if every word was some sort of warning. "I don't know what you're a doctor of, Dr. Bombfell," she told him curtly, "but adaptation doesn't seem to be your area of specialty."

Bombfell's volume grew, which Nebula assumed was for Croom's benefit more than hers. "I'll have you know I studied under the brilliant mind of Professor Quincy Buttersham in Mount Tumbledown's renowned Cultural Studies program. Have you heard of him?"

"I'm pleased to report that I have not."

"His paper on the adaptive hiding habits of long-surviving niche cultures was a cornerstone of the subject. Perhaps if your knowledge had more breadth and depth, you'd recognize him and his groundbreaking work."

Nebula stopped short of justifying his accusation. "I don't need to explain my opinions to you, Dr. Bombfell—or my education."

Croom was too consumed now with their discovery to hear their bickering. "Bringing back word that the Zingaloo still exist along with the Treasure Star will be such an amazing bonus for Hydewhite—and to think we'll have stayed a night in their hidden village. Such hospitality!"

Though she was reluctant to admit it even to herself, Nebula found his cool confidence and unwavering belief to be comforting, a balm to her unyielding sensibility and survivalist suspicion. "It is a very kind gesture on their part. We'll have a long climb ahead of us tomorrow, so I suppose we'd best camp down and—"

She was interrupted tersely by a band of tribesmen who emerged from the main cave pounding a drum, and another seven who emerged behind those, carrying a tremendous bowl filled with jungle fruits and flowers, seeds and nuts, berries and bushels of herbs.

"I do believe dinner is served!" Bombfell said.

The nightly banquet had been turned into a festival celebrating the tribe's new-found friends, which was a tad awkward considering that only one of them spoke Zingali with proficiency, while another fumbled with the language like a hot potato, and one spoke it not at all. But none of the three explorers realized how hungry they'd become until it dawned on them that they'd eaten the entire bowl among themselves and had left nothing for the rest of the tribe. There was more to be had, though—exotic fruits that tasted like blossoms, and an abundance of tasty seeds and nuts and berries that made the jerky and raisins they'd been subsisting on seem like tree bark and old spiders in comparison. It didn't seem to matter in the least that they'd gorged themselves; there was another bowl coming, and another one after that. And when they'd fattened themselves on the bounty of the jungle (as much as eating fruit and seeds can be considered "fattening up"), the young women of the tribe brought forth a great cone-shaped vessel that held an aromatic flower wine called *ploooip*, which Nebula politely declined in favor of keeping her wits about her, though she figured Croom and Bombfell wouldn't be nearly as refusing.

She was not incorrect.

Croom also wasn't the least bit shy when it came to chatting with the Zingaloo women, especially after guzzling three ladels of the wine; after all, he knew their native tongue now, and anything he said to them in Zingali couldn't have been half as confusing or offensive as what drunken things he might have said in English to women back home who would have understood him on the first try. Bombfell found his place with the older women of the tribe, who saw his silly, nonsensical conversation as the strange and witty concoctions of a mysterious traveler from an entirely different world than theirs.

Meanwhile, Nebula did her best to stand away from the hullabaloo, working on the ever-elusive cheek-flicking water doink sound that was key to speaking Zingali—a skill Croom had acquired without any practice at all—while everyone danced to their drunken hearts' content. A wayward tribal girl drifted in her direction and watched as she gave her sore cheek thump after thump, laughing uproariously every time the ripe-melon sound came from Nebula's mouth instead. The girl demonstrated with great care exactly how the sound was made. There were a few more futile attempts before Nebula had finally gathered enough finesse to pull it off. And once it happened, there was no stopping her. She and the girl shared a happy exchange of water doinks, which the girl found marvelously amusing, since it translated roughly to them pronouncing the letter C in English again and again.

It made Nebula far happier than it made the girl.

The great dish that had held their dinner was now lying near the fire, and the empty cone from which the wine had flowed had been turned on its bottom and stood up beside it; in other words, the tribe's dirty dishes were scattered all over the ground. But nobody seemed to mind as the stars salted the deep jungle sky and the celebration ran on into the wee hours.

"An acrobatic display of thanks to the tribe of the Zingaloo for their magnanimous hospitality!" Croom sang when he finally broke away from his bevy of Zingaloo lovelies, and then he sang it out in Zingali to make certain the message was received.

"Yes, yes!" Bombfell echoed. "They are a most hospitable tribe and deserve every wonderful glory that comes their way!" He attempted to say it in Zingali, but what came from his mouth was actually closer to, "I haven't seen the ocean recently, but I hear it's lovely in spring."

Then, as a result of a powerful tropical wine which turned out to have quite a bit more alcohol content than even Goodsense's bourbon, Croom took the opportunity to start in on his Chinese acrobatics without the least bit of hesitation. And Bombfell, being duly inspired by his friend, began turning crazy somersaults, much as he'd done in Murphy's Pub. Both were spinning wildly in their ridiculous contest again, heading in drunken revolutions toward the fire and the ceremonial pillar it surrounded. Before Nebula had a chance to race in their direction and warn them of how irresponsible they were being, they smashed broadly and cleanly into the pillar, their combined weight toppling it onto the torches. Then the two men themselves spilled over on top of it, landing in a heap as their carefree laughter turned to concerned cries of pain.

"What have you two done?!" Nebula called out.

"Well, I believe I've broken my mustache," Bombfell moaned as he rubbed his muzzle.

"And I don't think the cleft in my chin has ever seen such a sorry day," Croom groaned.

"None of which matters at all in light of the fact that you've toppled what appears to be a very important tribal totem!" she pointed out.

Chief Towhiit and the rest of the tribesmen ran to Croom and Bombfell, checking to make certain their guests weren't hurt. And Nebula, who'd taken quite a few steps back to give them space, saw the three stone pieces lying on the ground in sequence: the bowl, the pillar and the cone, and the image of it all came into focus for her. "Simeon...could you ask the chief in Zingali what significance the pillar holds?"

Croom did his best to wince out the question without causing further distress to his cleft.

The chief answered with a shrug of his shoulders and his eyebrows. *"Click-click-whitwhitwhit-POP-poppop-doink-doink-doink."*

"His toothless grandmother has told him the whole set is an heirloom that's been in their family for countless generations," Croom said with a sloppy, pained slur in his words. "It's called a skyclimber...it was once used to reach mangoes high in the treetops, but now they use it as a centerpiece for formal dining occasions such as this."

"Skyclimber..." Nebula said absently. To her sharp eye, it appeared to have far greater importance than the Zingaloo recognized. She grabbed the tablet and held it out alongside the scene before her to find the three shapes embossed upon it were laid out crookedly in their full three dimensions, in a form that could very well be taken to represent a rocket awaiting assembly.

She doinked her cheek in amazement.

EIGHT

It was half a day's journey down the Sarabezi River, and Simeon Croom and Horatio Bombfell had insisted on singing most of the morning. The selections switched easily from popular songs to church hymns, from opera to chorales, from radio jingles to show tunes. Nebula found that though she wasn't a fan of the song choices, Simeon did have a very nice singing voice, something akin to a baritone barber who'd abandoned his quartet. Bombfell, on the other hand, sounded like a bag of hammers falling down a sewer pipe filled with dying geese, if the geese had kazoos stuck in their throats.

The rest of his quartet had likely abandoned *him*.

It had taken a bit of Zingali sweet-talk for Croom to convince Chief Towhiit that the heirloom set were actually the pieces of the rocket that Thoiink had ridden to deliver the Treasure Star to the gods. But after the Zingaloo stopped laughing yet again at his ridiculous claim, the chief was persuaded to allow the explorers to lash the pillar, the ceremonial bowl, and the wine cone to the single-largest canoe the tribe possessed and paddle it down the Sarabezi, with tribesmen escorts as promised. Fortunately for all involved, the pieces were formed from Featherstone, which made them much easier to maneuver and carry down the river. Croom theorized that the potential discovery of Thoiink's Treasure Star would be such an easier task if they were to use the very rocket he used to set it in Heavencrest, which would more than make up for the time they'd lost on their Zingaloo village detour. And the chief was a reasonable man, even wearing his rubber tree plant crown-hat that made him look something like a rainforest court jester, though he still thought their endeavor of recreating what he considered to be a tribal fairy tale was futile. "*Cliiiiick-clickclick pop-pop-pop dowheeeep bloop-bloop-bloooooooop,*" he implored Croom, which translated to, "Just don't tell my grandmother about this... she'd kill me if she knew I let you take her centerpiece down the river."

Croom winked and assured the chief with a few water doinks that he would do his best to return everything in its original state before the old woman even realized it was missing.

So the troupe had loaded up at first light and set off in the crystal blue waters of the river, and were headed toward the sacred volcano Bazoot rather than to Heavencrest itself, with the sun shining its approval down on their journey. "If we're going to search for the star of the gods planted on the mountain by the Treasured One himself, we should follow his very path directly to the spot!" Croom said hopefully as he paddled the canoe.

Nebula was behind him doing her share of paddling, too. "Of course, you mean we should launch the rocket, watch where it lands, then follow its trajectory so we can search for the Treasure Star at its landing place," she said, with all the charmingly naïve logic of someone who'd never been on an adventure with Simeon Croom. "Don't you?"

"Of course I *don't*," Croom said definitively. "I mean that someone should ride the rocket to its destination to retrieve the relic."

"I couldn't agree more, Simeon—the rocket should be the vehicle used to reach the Treasure Star, if for no other reason than to maintain the time-honored legacy of intrepid courage in the name of discovery!" Bombfell exclaimed, as he reclined at the center of the canoe and did no paddling whatsoever.

"And I must absolutely be the one to pilot the craft," Croom affirmed as well. "After all, I have flown a barnstormer before, and I did minor in hang gliding for a while at Mount Tumbledown—long enough to acquire my operator's license, at least."

"How does any of that qualify you to pilot a rocket out of a volcano?" Nebula asked.

"Both involve flight, and both take place in the sky," Croom said over his shoulder.

"They're hardly comparable," Nebula protested.

"Be that as it may, I shall be the one." Croom said. He was fully in his element now.

Bombfell agreed to that too, naturally. "Yes...you should definitely be the one!"

Croom sang an aria about it, with a melody he made up on the spot. "I can hardly wait to find out what it feels like to a ride in an ancient stone rocket!" he boomed.

"It seems to me you'll be putting yourself in needless peril," Nebula continued. "Not to mention that we have only a vague idea of how the character in the myth performed this feat."

"I've been in equal peril on fraternity dares and party challenges, Neb," Croom assured her, "with absolutely *no* idea of what I was doing."

"Have you?" Nebula persisted. "Consider that we'll be entering an active volcano, assembling a stone vessel that we aren't certain is even capable of flight, and setting it atop a vent that could easily incinerate us with scorching steam, if not a flume of actual lava. And that's not to mention the dangers of riding on steam plumes which could be incredibly powerful, at elevations we can't predict. And the course it takes toward the mountain is—"

"So much naysaying!" Croom was in too good a mood to have it soured by Nebula's attempts at bringing him down. "It wouldn't kill you to believe a little more in the power of the ancient Zingaloo, would it?"

"No...but at some point, it might actually kill *you*."

Croom laughed his roguish adventurer laugh. "It's a chance I'm willing to take in the name of advancing our discovery of an ancient world that's been hidden away from us for two thousand years!"

"Well said!" Bombfell shouted.

Nebula found it entirely peculiar that, since their discovering the existence of the rocket, Bombfell—who'd never been at a loss for know-it-all interjections—had almost no new information to add to their narrative. He did nothing more than agree with his friend's every pronouncement, which made him seem even more unctuous and insincere than he'd seemed from the first. It put her on high alert and made her happy that she was sitting at the back of the canoe, where she could watch his every move. Unfortunately, his every move consisted only of him dragging his fingers through the cool water and whistling responses to the birds as they called out their morning songs. She was certain there were toxins leaching from his cold skin, tainting the Sarabezi and poisoning the wildlife.

And now, he appeared to have fallen asleep.

With Nebula being such a wet blanket and Bombfell providing no musical accompaniment anymore, Croom began chatting in crackly click-pop Zingali, describing in tremendous and unnecessary detail some of his more incredible exploits to the Zingaloo canoe crew, who erupted every so often in bubbly laughter, or a chorus of *ooooohs* if the situation called for it. "I believe I've found my perfect audience, Neb," Croom crowed.

"Give them a few minutes more," she said sourly. "I'm sure they'll come to their senses."

By midday, they'd reached the shore that Bazoot loomed over, his grand crater exhaling fumes like a stony monarch blowing smoke rings into the cloud-strewn sky over his head. "Are we in danger of an eruption?" Nebula asked. "The smoke seems significantly more plumed than it did yesterday..."

Croom *click-pop-doinked* the question to the Zingaloo. "Our guides are happy to report that Bazoot has been sleeping soundly for ages. The vapor jets are all he's had to offer for years...they wouldn't expect an eruption for a very long time."

"Oh. That's a relief."

Croom smirked. "But who knows? Anything is possible." He always liked to leave enough room in his adventures for the unknown to keep excitement high until the very end. He frequently did the same with museum deadlines and birthday shopping for his mother. Unlikely though it seemed, all of these situations were fraught with equal danger.

As both a partner to his adventure and his last-minute mother-birthday-shopper, Nebula was amused by neither.

The tribesman carried the pieces off the canoe, hauled it easily up the riverbank, and lugged it handily to the knurled, rippling base of Bazoot. Finding a way in to the caverns below the volcano proved to be something of a challenge, but it was nothing a trio of well-traveled, well-trained, and well-educated explorers couldn't handle... though, since Bombfell had become increasingly lazy during the walk, he insisted on keeping watch for "jungle cats and thieving bandits" by bringing up the rear rather than making a true contribution, which meant there was really only a duo explorers engaged in the search. Croom, as good-natured as ever, didn't seem to mind the imbalance, but it only added to Nebula's dislike of his friend.

"Simeon," Nebula began quietly as they carefully negotiated the sharp volcanic rock in search of a portal inward, "was Bombfell always this unhelpful on your excursions?"

Croom brushed it off a bit too easily. "Oh, Neb; surely you know how it goes with these things: sometimes you lead, and sometimes you follow. It's inherent in being part of a crew."

"Yes, but while we circle back and forth searching for passage, he's leaning against a tree, which is neither leading nor following but something much closer to napping. It doesn't feel as if he's pulling his weight...if feels as if we pull it for him. And his weight is quite considerable."

"He does seem a little...disengaged, doesn't he?" Croom mused aloud.

"No; he seems *entirely* disengaged. He also seems..."

"Cranky?" Croom offered.

"Acerbic," Nebula corrected him, "thoroughly unpleasant at times...and downright inconsiderate of us both."

Croom wondered if maybe his old friend was honestly, finally tuckering out. "Perhaps he's right; perhaps this will be his last adventure ever."

"His," Nebula asked solemnly, "but not yours?"

"I honestly cannot say for certain, Neb," Croom said with that familiar, wistful glimmer in his voice. "This experience has sparked my interest in discovering the world again. My engine is revving for this sort of excursion now, perhaps like it never has before. I'm not sure how I'll be able to go back to museum life after this."

His words sent a coin of discontent chiming into the well of Nebula's happiness as she pictured a Hydewhite devoid of Simeon Croom and his charming, arrogant, oblivious, and at times all-out-brilliant energy. "Oh. Well...I suppose it was worth doing after all, then, especially if you find the Treasure Star and bring it back to Hydewhite. You'll have the glory and the satisfaction, and you can be off around the world again, and everyone concerned will be all the better for it." The words may have been encouraging, but the tone was anything but.

Croom was then, as he always was, entirely unaware of the true sentiment Nebula was hinting at. "It would be a perfect situation, wouldn't it? A bloody brilliant point to mark the ending of one career, and the advent of another that blends the old with the new."

"How wonderful it would be for you," Nebula managed to say, and though she was being entirely genuine about it, she couldn't help but hear the disappointment in her own voice.

"Wonderful for us all, perhaps!" Croom sang as his fingers found a curvature in the surface of Bazoot that led inward along a curving path that smelled of sulfur, smoke, and possibility. "Tliktlik," Croom called out to the canoe captain in pops and clicks, "have the men bring the rocket pieces this way. I believe we've found our entrance."

"So you have!" Bombfell said, suddenly and softly appearing at their side.

Nebula gave a startled croak at his unannounced presence.

"Isn't it splendid, friend?" Croom sang out.

"Oh, it is," Bombfell replied greasily. "And utterly so."

⚬

The cavern beneath Bazoot was something of a mezzanine that overlooked a roiling lava pool; a crusty black skin covered the magma, breaking open lazily in oozing red-orange bubbles to breathe out white-hot steam and add to the seething heat. And above their heads was the great throat of the grand old man, extending high into the jungle and above the canopy outside. The far side of the platform featured a fair-sized hole that emitted steamy curls of vapor and every so often huffed tiny clusters of ash into the air. A spot of blue sky and sunlight shone in from high above at a slight bias—an opening presumed to be the exit point through which Thoiink made his flight, though presumption wasn't such a comforting phenomenon in such a precarious situation.

It was all they had in their favor at the moment.

"Astounding," Croom uttered. "It's as if we're living out Thoiink's story, following in the footsteps of the ancients!"

Nebula herself was stunned as she imagined a mythical character from the prehistory of this mysterious tribe hoping to appease his divinity by soaring through a hole in a volcanic tube with a star-gift in his possession. "How hopeful he must have been at this moment," she said, "how filled with optimism and dread at the same time."

"I'll say," Croom agreed.

"We stand on the shoulders of the gods, my friends!" Bombfell said melodramatically as he dabbed the sweat from his forehead. "Or in the footprints of those who sought to appease them, at least."

"I hope it ends up being worth all the risk," Nebula said, refusing to give the man even a scrap of credit.

"How could it not, Neb?" Croom asked. "The tablet has led us here—to the Zingaloo, to the rocket, to Bazoot. We need only aim for the peak and find the Treasure Star, and we'll be the absolute rage of the anthropology world."

Nebula wasn't certain the anthropology world even had the capacity for rage-level of excitement. But far be it from her to crush his dream.

The Zingaloo crew worked to assemble the rocket into a single structure centered over the hole as Croom laid out his plan. "Let's presume that Thoiink crammed himself into the cone by climbing into the tube...and that the tube rested on the inverted dish as a lifter. Unless he was a fair amount smaller than I am, there should be just enough room for me and my parachute for safe landings wherever I might end up. Then, I'll poke around a while until I find the orb, I'll gather it up safely, and I'll parachute back down to the banks of the Sarabezi, where my dear and loyal friends await my descent."

In addition to the geography charts she'd memorized, Nebula had made incredible mental notes regarding the intended region of Heavencrest as they passed it while paddling down the Sarabezi. "There seems to be soft canopy along the entire ridge that should cushion the rocket no matter where it lands, though the foliage could hide a more treacherous terrain up there."

"Another swan dive into the unknown for us, Simeon!" Bombfell said happily, as if he were the one taking the chance and all too ready to put his neck on the line, even though it was currently seeping sweat into the collar of his khaki shirt and had no intention of finding itself in a rocket made of stone built two thousand years prior.

"And what will *you* be sacrificing for this discovery, Dr. Bombfell?" Nebula asked. "I don't hear you volunteering life or limb, and you certainly haven't been forthcoming with your assistance in getting us to this point."

"Don't be so hard on the man," Croom said, in the manner of defending his friend that was now becoming a nuisance to Nebula. "He's made his contribution: he brought us the tablet, and the mythology, and the knowledge of this most surprising tribe as bestowed upon him by Dr. Twill. Without Horatio, we wouldn't even know about the Treasure Star of the Zingaloo, let alone stand possibly moments away from finding it and claiming it for Hydewhite!"

"She's right, Simeon," Bombfell protested, in a surprising turn of events. "Perhaps I haven't given enough. Perhaps I should be the one sent up in the rocket. There's a tremendous chance that you won't survive this, and you shouldn't sacrifice your life in service of a cause you had no idea existed before I arrived."

It sounded like far too leading a statement, and Nebula had a sneaking suspicion that this had all been rehearsed long ago, that the majority of their adventures together ended in a similar fashion, with Croom doing all the legwork and Bombfell reveling in the overspill of glory without having undertaken even a fraction of the labor. She just knew that Bombfell's protest was all for Croom's benefit, and that there was no sincerity at all in what he said.

"No, Horatio; it shall be me," Croom insisted. "No reason for you to tire yourself further."

Bombfell appeared to force a blush, though it was just as likely a result of the volcanic heat. "You are a good friend indeed, Simeon."

Croom smiled. "It's my third-greatest feature."

"I thought you said your humility was your third-greatest feature," Nebula reminded him, with all the irony such a statement could afford.

"Ah yes!" Croom laughed. "Well, it's just moved down the list!"

Nebula was far too concerned with his well-being at the moment to find humor in that.

Croom tapped his trusty machete, strapped firmly to his thigh. "If there is a Treasure Star to be found up there, Doris and I will find it. Wish me well, friends—see you on the other side of things!" he cried happily. And then he was off, walking across the mezzanine with his parachute strapped tightly to his back like a turtle shell. He scaled the tube with the same dexterity he'd used to climb the Waliki tree, and he tucked himself into the cylinder before sliding the nose cone on top of it. Then Tliktlik and the other Zingaloo tribesmen angled the rocket at a proper bias for blast off. All that was needed now was a little volcanic boost from Bazoot.

"How long before it takes off, do you think?" Bombfell asked as he watched the rocket, his eyes searching and severe, his voice as dry as paper.

Nebula was loathe to answer him. "The vapor plumes appear to erupt in ten minute intervals. We should see another in the next two minutes or so."

"Excellent," he purred.

"You eagerness for this seems a tad too self-serving, Dr. Bombfell," Nebula pointed out.

"And your distaste for me has become unmistakable, Miss Everhope," Bombfell said, sere and unfriendly. "I don't think I like it very much."

Nebula was in no mood to fake manners. "I'm hardly concerned with your likes."

"You'd do best to not fall entirely out of my favor," he warned her.

"I wonder if Simeon recognizes at all that his oldest, dearest friend doesn't exactly have his best interests at heart," she said casually. "He is putting his life on the line for this quest, after all."

Bombfell's eyes slid from the rocket, which was now trembling under the building heat of the plume, toward Nebula. He spoke to her menacingly, without turning his head. "Simeon knows exactly who he's in league with, and he has for quite some time now. I can't be held responsible for his shortcoming if he fails to remember that at the moment."

Nebula was incredulous. "Who in blazes are you, Dr. Bombfell?"

"I'm a man of greater significance than you'll ever appreciate." He was unapologetic about everything now.

It made her blood boil.

"Now if you'll excuse me," Bombfell said curtly. "The heat from this blasted volcano is making my knees sweat, and I've had just about enough of this madness to last me the rest of my life." Then he turned and walked out of the tunnel to watch the launch from the jungle instead.

Nebula's stomach tightened as she watched him go, wondering which was the greater danger now: Croom's perilous rocket ride to a precarious peak, or Bombfell waiting like a slippery reptile to catch him when he parachuted into the river valley below.

She followed the ominous mystery of a man out of the volcano, her concern pushing her at a hasty pace.

NINE

Croom was smooshed into the cylinder sardine-style, sweating like a sponge wrung out after a hot bath, waiting for the launch in whatever form it might take. It wasn't a long wait, but for a man as anxious and excited by the prospect of taking a rocket ride as Croom was, it seemed an excruciating eternity. He whistled a triumphant tune, something he imagined would accompany such a momentous occasion as this one. He tapped his fingers against the wall of the stone cylinder, drumming them thumb-to-pinky, then pinky-to-thumb, then thumb-to-pinky again. He took a good long glance through the small portal carved in the side of the wall, which he presumed would give him an opportunity to line up his exit from the rocket when he was over the landing point, but all he could see was steam. Then he spoke to himself, presumably because there was no one else crushed in the tube to hear him, and also because he reasoned his voice would sound supremely rich and resonant in a hollowed-out stone tube, and he didn't want to miss out on the only chance he might have to hear it. "I suppose it'll be a while before—"

In a screeching roar that sounded and smelled like a dragon choking on a pipe filled with rotten eggs, the sulfurous steam intensified.

Then, as anticipated, the vapor jet erupted.

The entire craft shuddered as it soared up the throat of the volcano, though it quickly became a supremely smooth *whooooosh* skyward once it evacuated Bazoot. It moved at an incredibly high velocity, though it felt nothing like the aircraft he was familiar with. Whenever Croom had flown—even when he'd hang-glided or taken the yoke of the blue barnstormer he'd reminisced about with Bombfell—he had always been in an environment that could be governed by a pilot or an engine or a propeller. In this instance, he was at the whim of steam propulsion and the mercy of gravity.

He could only hope the rocket was sturdy enough to hold together two thousand years after its initial launch.

Though the Featherstone made it considerably light, it wasn't weightless, a fact made even more evident with the added weight of Croom wedged within. But when the rocket reached its apex, it hung in the sky, suspended like a star itself for the briefest of moments. Croom looked through the small portal window, watching the incredible view of the Sarabezi and its surrounding jungle, like a photographic post card from someone else's vacation voyage. He imagined the scrolling cursive *Wish you were here!* printed across the bottom, and he was ever so glad in his adventurer's heart, in his explorer's brain, and in his eternally-twelve-year-old smile that he *was* there.

"This is what the gods must see of us when they gaze down upon the world," he said, a spot of genuine humility glinting in his eye.

Then gravity tapped its toe, and the rocket began plummeting back to earth, with a wistful, awestruck Simeon Croom still crammed inside.

⚓

Nebula and the Zingaloo tribesmen stood below the volcano, watching as the rocket sailed high into the sapphire sky and made an elegant arc toward Heavencrest. Bombfell stood away from them, watching the same scene with what appeared to be more fervid attention than he'd shown during most of the journey. It didn't escape Nebula's notice. "Off you go to find our lovely prize," he said flaccidly, as if he was talking to himself.

"Aren't you worried that he won't land safely, Dr. Bombfell?" Nebula asked angrily. "Aren't you the least bit concerned that your dear friend might crash before he's able to find your precious artifact?"

"Simeon Croom is the most capable, danger-evading soul I've ever encountered," Bombfell said. His voice had finally shed every bit of its falsely friendly melody. "There is no one in the world better equipped to survive a ride in an ancient stone rocket toward a mountain peak."

"Then we should head toward the base of the mountain to be there when he parachutes down, shouldn't we?" she said icily.

"Of course we should," Bombfell agreed with great indignation, "so we can see the Treasure Star when he retrieves it for me."

"For *you*?" Nebula asked. "What exactly is your intention in all of this, Dr. Bombfell?"

Bombfell didn't bother answering. He simply began the trek without another word, slithering into the undergrowth while Nebula worked with her broken Zingali to inform Tliktlik that she would be back shortly with Croom, whether or not the artifact had been found. But the tribesman had already begun running in the direction of the rocket's path to collect the pieces so they could be returned before dinner; otherwise, there'd be nothing to carry the fruit in, and the wine couldn't be properly made without the nose cone. So Nebula set off toward the mountain alone, watching Bombfell's path and following behind him as closely as she could.

Meanwhile, the rocket reached its zenith in the sky, hanging for a scant second and appearing to stop entirely mid-flight.

Nebula Everhope felt her heart do the very same thing.

Then the rocket tilted nose-down and readied to make its fall back to land.

~∞~

Croom kicked off the nose cone, tucked and rolled out of the stone cylinder into the bare sky, and pulled his rip-cord just as the pinnacle of the mountain range came into view beneath him. "For history, antiquity, reknown!" he bellowed, though of course, as far up in the atmosphere as he was, no one could actually hear him. Then his parachute blossomed overhead like a great mushroom cap and swallowed a great gulp of wind in its billow. He made the lazy, swaying descent over the Sarabezi, a picture-perfect drop into yet another cluster of lush foliage, this one with such a rich, unexplored tangle of primeval wildness, he questioned whether he'd be able to find the Treasure Star at all, even if it *was* up there.

He saw the trees coming up quickly now, though there wasn't much he could do to slow himself. So he braced himself as he neared the ground, buckled his knees, and rolled six times along the high jungle floor until he came to a sudden stop against a boulder. Thankfully, his impact was cushioned by the chute, which had wrapped around him like a cocoon.

He slowly disentangled himself, disconnected from his chute and his pack, and surveyed the mountain. The peak had very little space through which to wander about, and sheer drops down into the jungle canopy on every side. It likely hadn't been explored by humans since Thoiink purposely aimed himself here to bring his gift to the gods. Croom took out his trusty machete and began slashing through the undergrowth for something that looked like the bejeweled stone sphere that Bombfell had described. "It can't be that difficult to find, can it, Doris?" he asked his machete. "Certainly no more challenging than taking a rip-roaring rocket ride on a volcanic plume." Croom felt about beneath the large leaves and between the soft grasses as if he were searching for an Easter egg, but instead found three families of frogs, a bevy of lizards, and a cluster of rocks that were as unbejeweled as stone could possibly be. They were also covered in slime, which, of all the strange challenges he'd encountered so far, seemed to be the one that unsettled him the most. "Utterly disgusting," he said, wiping his hands clean on an oversized leaf. "If I were a mortal hoping to appease a sky filled with angry gods by placing a jeweled star-orb offering high enough for it to catch the glint of the sun when my fellow tribesmen looked at these mountains...where would I put it?" Croom mused as he stroked his chin. "Somewhere as high as possible, most likely." He craned his neck to see the height of the trees towering above him, far higher than the Waliki tree he and Nebula had climbed before the Zingaloo caught them. But it was nowhere near as high as the highest tree he'd ever climbed. "Up we go, then," he said, strapping Doris back in her holster as he began making his way up the great tree trunk in monkey-like fashion. And when he discovered nothing at the top of that one, he simply stepped onto the branches of the neighboring tree, which intertwined with the branches of the other tree like a braided rope. And when he reached the extent of that tree and found there to be nothing but sloths and frustration, he leapt into the arms of the next tree over. He traveled from tree to tree like this, leaping to some, slithering into others, until he'd crossed the tree tops of the entire peak, but he found no evidence of anything like a treasure, let alone one that could be mistaken for a star.

"There has to be something here...hasn't there?" Croom began realizing that with its sheer vertical facing, its remote location, and its thoroughly untouched and savage wilderness, there was no chance of anyone else making the ascent, no possibility of someone else having absconded with the relic at any time in the past. It was simply too unreachable by anyone but the bravest of souls, with the least possible regard for his own personal safety. In the world of exploring and adventure, Croom knew the list of those people was incredibly brief, and he was at the top of it in his day. So if there were indeed treasure to be found in Heavencrest, it would still be there somewhere, and he would be the one to find it...and yet, there he was, in the midst of the mountaintop, empty-handed and growing light-headed from the altitude and the exertion. But there was mounting evidence regarding the artifact that simply couldn't be denied: the rocket existed, the tablet map had led him here, and Bazoot had done its share getting him up the mountain. There was nothing left to prove other than the Treasure Star itself.

But it seemed to be the most hidden mystery of all.

"We haven't come all this way for nothing, have we, old man?" he asked himself. "If it isn't in the trees, then it's in the underbrush somewhere. Let's recover this treasure and fall back to earth to celebrate with friends, shall we?" he asserted. Then he kissed his machete's blade for luck, and his search ramped up to a pace somewhere between racing to find something sweet to eat during a low blood sugar attack during his last great adventure before this one, and trying to evade the swarm of bees that besieged him after he'd attacked their hive in search of honey to do just that.

He was practically a blur.

He swished and swooped and swung, clobbering the very forces of nature that had allowed the land to grow itself into a lacework of tendrils and blooms and rough-skinned vines. He seemed tireless now, as if there was nothing that could stop him until he either discovered what he was searching for, or his arm fell off, both of which were equally likely outcomes judging by his exaggerated motions. And then, when he'd nearly hacked the entire mountain top into clippings, his machete clanged against something that rang out in a pitch he identified as high A, and his swinging arm vibrated in sympathy to the tone. "Great guardians of the cosmos, Doris," he said in an astonished hush as he pushed the overgrowth aside. His face lit up even brighter than the object he was looking at. "I think we've finally hit upon something."

❦

In the steamy tropical valley below, Bombfell moved at what seemed like a ridiculously speedy clip for someone who'd claimed to be too exhausted to help carry a canoe—or to row it, for that matter—while Nebula nipped at his heels, her busy, suspicious mind racing with all sorts of diabolical scenarios for why they were really on this voyage. She heard his voice up ahead, and a static-filled crackling that could have been either the snapping of branches under heavy boot heels...or a walkie-talkie.

"You won't get the better of me, Dr. Bombfell," Nebula swore under her breath. "Not you, and certainly not your sweaty knees."

There was nothing now but a swath of foliage and a curtain of mist between Nebula and Bombfell, and more of the same between Bombfell and the base of the mountain. Nebula was extra-vigilant, keeping watch for the telltale sign of Croom's chute blossoming in the sky as she ran so she could reach him before his so-called friend did when he finally landed.

And it happened before she realized it.

There was a call of, "*Adventurer niiiigh, falling from the skyyyyy!*" and Simeon Croom came crashing through the canopy nearly one hundred feet ahead of her...which put him only fifty feet ahead of Bombfell. So she doubled her pace and tore toward him as fast as the jungle would allow her to go, which wasn't terribly fast now that the underbrush had thickened. She was faced with snarls underfoot and vines overhead, and inhospitable barbed tendrils reaching out for her from all sides, and either hissing, rattling, or buzzing from the creatures that lingered near no matter where she turned.

"Did you find it, Simeon?" she heard Bombfell say with his artificial sing-song good will. "Did you find the Treasure Star?"

"I certainly did!" Croom said. His parachute had tangled in the trees just enough to leave his feet dangling above the ground. "And even after two thousand years of being grown over with treacherous jungle vegetation, it's a lovely wonder to behold!"

Nebula crashed through the jungle just behind them, fully out of breath but determined to not drop her guard in Bombfell's presence for even a second. She did her best to communicate this with her eyebrows, but even those were exhausted and made sloppy, sliding shapes instead of offering anything comprehensible.

"Then end the suspense, my friend!" Bombfell exclaimed. "Show us the relic!"

Croom reached behind himself and produced a breathtaking blue-opal globe that fit squarely in his palm, his fingers clawed tightly to contain it. It was run through with sparkling golden streaks that seemed to be electrically charged, glowing within from some vibrant power. "Miraculous, wouldn't you say, Horatio?"

"Dear mercy..." All the breath in Bombfell's considerable lungs left him in the course of a single, overwhelmed sigh. "It's like staring into the eyes of the gods themselves," he said, nearly in a whisper. "May I hold it?"

"Well, of course you can! We wouldn't even have it without you." He tossed the gem down into Bombfell's greasy hands.

Bombfell rubbed the blue-opal globe on his sleeve until it shone like daylight. He watched veins of golden energy waver beneath the surface, his eyes flickering as if he were falling into a strange hypnotic daze. "Sheer beauty... at long last."

"Simeon..." Nebula huffed finally, "...I don't think... you'll want to..."

Before she could gather enough breath to finish warning Croom about what his so-called friend was actually up to, Bombfell changed character entirely. He dropped the globe into his pocket, and with his free hand drew a pistol, which was essentially no surprise to Nebula after what she'd seen from him, but which seemed to take Croom quite aback.

"Horatio, what is the meaning of this?" Croom barked.

"Perhaps I should have informed you from the beginning, Simeon," Bombfell told him plainly, "but I'm not in the business of adventure for free anymore...my services come at a price now."

"Services?" Croom said gruffly. "But we were doing this for the sake of Hydewhite, and for our own shared sense of adventure...weren't we?"

"Oh, we were indeed, my friend. But that was only one layer of the pie."

Nebula finally regained her voice enough to speak in full sentences without depending on her facial features to finish her thoughts. "Pies don't have layers, you moron!" she said.

Bombfell let loose a deep, troubling laugh, and Nebula wondered how he'd come by a trait so tell-tale and convincing when everything else about him had seemed so designed to deceive from the start. "Well, this one does, Miss Everhope...and we've barely broken through the crust."

"Maybe you could explain yourself without making a food analogy, Horatio," Croom requested. "And a bit more quickly, if you would. My legs are going numb in this harness."

A shadow slowly crossed in front of the sun, and for a brief moment, Nebula wondered if the gods had been angered by their unclaimed offering being taken away so abruptly by a trio of trespassing troublemakers in their jungle.

"I'll say only this, Simeon," Bombfell said. "Regardless of the underlying purpose in acquiring the Treasure Star, I truly hold our friendship dear, and I hope you do the same. I do understand if my sudden self-serving shift on behalf of the agency that employs me means you can no longer trust me. But know that I meant it when I said I could never have done this without you, old friend."

"This is how you treat someone you call a friend?" Nebula asked angrily.

Bombfell arched an eyebrow, which fit perfectly with his lecherous sneer. "Unfortunately, *my dear*, it is now."

A rope ladder unrolled from the shadow above them, and Nebula craned her neck to see that the shadow wasn't cast by the gods at all, but the super-silent dirigible that had carried them to the Sarabezi sliding into station over the canopy. "The people I work for will be ever so pleased to learn that the Treasure Star of the Zingaloo is now where it properly belongs. Things couldn't have fallen into place more perfectly."

With a deft flick of his wrist, Croom snapped the straps of his chute open and dropped into a smooth tuck-and-roll on the jungle floor below. Then he swept his leg wide in an attempt to kick Bombfell's feet out from under him. But Bombfell anticipated his friend's logic far too well, and he leapt high to avoid taking a tumble. "I've worked too hard and come too far for this just to have it ruined by your unrelenting sense of goodness, Simeon! There's a greater dynamic at play here, with further reaching implications than you could possibly understand."

"I don't know how you've grown so corrupt, Horatio," Croom replied, dropping into a defensive wrestling stance, "but I can't let you get away with whatever you have planned."

Suddenly, they were at it again, swinging and twirling in what threatened to be a repeat of their contest at Murphy's pub.

Meanwhile, the shadow over them darkened, and the dirigible loomed larger and closer.

Croom crouched low and watched carefully as Bombfell swung a boot in a high curve aimed right at his chin, but he spun and ducked just in time to avoid a heel-chop to his charming cleft. And while Bombfell was preoccupied righting himself from the near-miss, Croom leapt high and reached for an overhanging branch above them, the perfect height for him to catch his opponent in the chest with a well-landed double-donkey front kick. His boot heels landed squarely against his friend's breastplate, sending him sprawling back against a Waliki tree behind him. The gun flew from his hand, skittering into the underbrush.

"I wouldn't want to hurt you, Horatio," Croom said, now on a single knee in a pose that made it appear he could uncoil and spring as high as he needed to.

"It's entirely possible that you'll have to, Simeon," Bombfell said, regaining his breath as he stood upright again. "But it isn't very likely you'll be able to."

Then Bombfell jumped high with his arms above his head and flew in Croom's direction like a wrestler off of a turnbuckle. Croom could hardly dive out of the way quickly enough to avoid being flattened. It was only by the luck of his well-practiced grace that he missed the crushing weight of Bombfell and his voluminous mustache.

Bombfell rolled twice and bounced back onto his feet, turning in a single spin to face Croom yet again. "En garde!"

he cried, his hands raised flat and straight like blades before him.

Croom mirrored his actions, though his came with a deep crease of the brow and a cocky, charismatic smirk that Bombfell was nowhere near skilled enough to pull off. "Let's see what else you've got!"

And then, the martial arts segment of their hand-to-hand combat began...

"This might never end," Nebula said to herself as she watched them spinning and chopping toward each other, each too agile and perceptive to make contact though they truly were giving it their best. So she did the only thing she thought might bring their confrontation to an end, even though it was fool-hearty and ill-advised.

Believing it would interrupt their brawl, she closed her eyes and stepped between the two men.

Bombfell spun with an open hand and landed a slap against her cheek, the sound of which was painfully resounding, and the impact of which sent her falling aside with her teeth chattering and a welt in the shape of Bombfell's horrible handprint rising on her skin.

"Neb!" Croom shouted. His display of battle moves shifted immediately into rescue mode as he dove in her direction and caught her in a dip before she hit the ground. "Are you all right?"

"I...think I am," she said, her spinning eyes finding focus on the cleft in Croom's chin.

"If he's hurt you seriously, I'll never forgive him." Croom's voice was low and sincere.

"If you let him escape, I'll never forgive *you*," Nebula said, pointing to Bombfell.

The hit was enough of a distraction to allow Bombfell to reach for the rope ladder that had fallen from the dirigible. He stepped onto the rungs and looped his elbow tightly around the rope as it hauled him up through the trees, the glimmering blue orb held aloft like a trophy in his free hand. "An honorable fellow to the very end, Simeon, and a hero worthy of the swooning damsel in your arms!"

"You villainous traitor!" Croom called after him. "You treacherous snake!"

"Flattery will get you nowhere...you should know that by now," Bombfell shouted down at him, shaking the orb to add insult to injury. "*Au revoir, mon ami*!" The dirigible rose and took its shadow with it, leaving Simeon Croom in the Sarabezi jungle with Nebula Everhope in his arms, rising to a frothing rage at the betrayal by his horrible, sweaty friend as he flew away.

"Simeon – we can't let him get away!" Nebula cried, on her feet again.

"I'm afraid we have no choice, Neb," Croom said calmly. "He has a blimp, and we have...well, what do we have?"

"Nothing, Simeon—we have nothing!" Nebula had never been so angry with him, and he'd once accidentally set her hair aflame while making a grilled cheese sandwich in the museum break room.

"Really?" Croom questioned. "Nothing at all?"

"Nothing! We made every ounce of the discovery that occurred on this trip," she raved, "and you hand him the relic like it was a bottle of brandy to take with him on his evil airship!" She was beyond incensed now, reaching the point of sheer frustrated surrender. "He's been your friend for ages, and you couldn't tell that he might—he *just might*—be double-crossing you, with his lazy lack of assistance, and his arrogant, haughty ways, and his inability to speak a language his mentor taught him?"

"Well, now," Croom said calmly. "When you put it that way, he does sound like something of a heel, doesn't he?"

His understatement didn't amuse her in the least. "I don't know why you ever trusted him on this excursion!"

"And why would you assume that I did?" Croom asked.

Nebula's furious eyes could have launched poisoned darts. "Because you let him bring us all this way only to escape with the Treasure Star!"

"Oh, Neb...you know me better than that." Croom walked back to his parachute pack, still hanging in the tree. "I believe Horatio said it best himself when he told you trust is a currency we spend sparingly when in the depths of adventure. True that I let him bring us all this way on little more than a scrap of evidence that there was even a relic worth chasing, but I would never in a million years allow him to take the Treasure Star."

"I...don't understand," Nebula said.

"Perhaps this will explain it better." Croom reached into his pack and produced what looked to be a tarnished golden cannonball. "I wouldn't exactly call it 'nothing', and I'm guessing you won't, either."

Nebula's eyes grew large at the sight of the orb. She brushed away a bit of the crust that had developed around it during its time in the jungle and felt its sleek, smooth texture. There were strange symbols pressed into the surface of it around its center, like a belt, pictograms that looked far more sophisticated than what the Zingaloo tablet had shown, and arranged at intervals around the top hemisphere were rotund blue-opal jewels identical to the one Croom had given Bombfell, with a single empty setting where he'd pulled that one free. "You gave him a piece of the star instead of the whole thing..."

Croom smirked. "Horatio Bombfell may be a lifelong friend, and he and I may have circled the world in search of adventure together, but he has never been someone deserving of my full confidence. He always had a hidden agenda the times before, and clearly he had one this time as well."

Nebula nodded. "Well, now it appears that an outside influence has guided this entire excursion, thanks to him."

"Yes...it does appear that way." Croom seemed genuinely troubled for the first time on the journey, as if the adventure was all finished up and had left behind more of a mystery than it had solved.

"Still, it's an amazing collection of discoveries you've made, Simeon, the whole 'betrayed by Bombfell' element notwithstanding," Nebula said as she took the orb from his hands, turned it over, and examined every inch of it. "Hydewhite will be so pleased."

"Well...perhaps they will, and perhaps they won't."

Nebula was confused, a look she didn't wear frequently, and one which didn't suit her one bit. "How is it even possible that they wouldn't love what you've found?"

Croom ruminated aloud as he took back the artifact, a practice he'd picked up while teaching a course in the relevance of antiquity in the modern era, as well as by watching detective serials at the cinema. "Until Horatio made his approach, we hadn't even heard of the Zingaloo, let alone their magical language or their mythical sky-climber Thoiink...by the time we knew anything of them, they were believed to be an extinct culture, lost to the world forever, save for their study by Dr. Twill—whose existence is in great question now, I might add. Our expedition has not only revealed them to be a living, breathing tribal society whose beliefs and practices have evolved over centuries, but a source of truth in mythology, which is something so rare and wonderful it's only happened a handful of times in any of the vast range of cultures I've studied."

It was a rare occasion during which Simeon Croom's thinking couldn't be unwoven by the deft mind of Nebula Everhope. This happened to be one of them. "I'm not sure I see where you're heading with this."

"I believe the discovery of the Zingaloo may have to suffice as our prize to Hydewhite, and perhaps some lesser artifact we can convince them to part with, something significant that confirms their existence; the fact that we've located a long-lost tribe and brought back *any* piece of their long-surviving culture should justify their investment." Croom rubbed his chin and gazed down at the orb as if it were a baby asleep in his arms. "This artifact, however, will be not be leaving the Sarabezi jungle."

"But the reason they allowed you to come at all was to collect the Treasure Star without knowing for certain that it even existed," Nebula reminded him. "And now you've not only proven that it does, you've actually located it, and at no small peril in the process. Why wouldn't we bring it back?"

"Because it doesn't *belong* to us, Neb. It belongs to the tribe. The Zingaloo are no longer some mysterious culture long-extinct, but a living, breathing people who've managed to blend in so well with their environment that they've evaded detection for two millennia. They're a link to the ancient world, and that in itself must be treasure enough."

While Croom's reasoning was sound, it was difficult to validate his timing, and Nebula wasn't entirely convinced.

His sense of nobility, however, was noteworthy, though she stopped short of complimenting him on it. "Are you sure this is the best approach to take?"

Croom was unwavering. "I'm thoroughly positive about it. To us, the star is an artifact; to them, it's an heirloom that bridges the gap between their past and their present. It's their treasure to keep, not ours to take."

"I can't say your feelings are wrong, Simeon. I just hope the museum sees things the same way."

"Yes...they can be a sticky lot." Croom's deep consideration of this forced his eyebrows in two different directions. "I'll do my persuasion thing with them again. I'm sure it'll be fine."

Nebula could think of at least seven other instances in their time together when he'd uttered that very same phrase. At least four of them had ended with an ambulance ride, and two required a written apology.

At the moment, however, she could do little else but agree.

❧

Thikthik and the other Zingaloo tribesmen were waiting by the bank of the Sarabezi when Croom and Nebula finally found their way back to the river. The pieces of the rocket had already been loaded onto the canoe; they were readying the wheeled platform that would haul the whole load back to the village over land when Croom showed them the Treasure Star. The frothing *click-pop-doink* chatter that arose when they saw the orb became a deafening rush alive with unmitigated excitement. And when the explorers returned to the village and Chief Towhiit saw that the star was a real item and no longer just an element from a children's story, his eyes glowed with wonder and surprise. Croom explained that the star wasn't quite where Thoiink had left it in the myth, that it hadn't been claimed by the star gods as the tribe had come to believe and therefore was the Zingaloo's treasure to do with what they pleased. "*Click-dink-doing-click-click-pop!*" the chief said, which Croom loosely translated to Nebula as meaning, "Hallelujah!" Towhiit summoned the crowd with a frantic waving of his hands. They followed him to the river, where he sank the orb and washed it clean of the dirt and debris that had gathered over so many centuries, and when it was finally clean, it shone like a midday sun in their midst. Then he rolled the star over in his hands, laughing all the while. At the front of the orb was the impression of a shape sunk in low relief in the very center of its metallic skin. It was something of a circle with six triangles stationed around its outer edge; a smaller sunken circle filled its center, with a ray extending through the bottom of the circle. A split arrowhead formed the end of the ray.

Croom watched over his shoulder. "It's the same symbol that's pressed into the tablet," he said thoughtfully. "The symbol of the gods."

Chief Towhiit pressed on the symbol until it gave a gentle *click*. The whole tribe circled around with bright, open eyes, watching as the orb began emitting a droning hum in three harmonic tones, like a choir of angelic voices repeating in a droning hum what sounded to be the word *shtaaaAAAaaa... shtaaaAAAaaa... shtaaaAAAaaa...*

"Shtaaa," Nebula said softly, recognizing the sound of it. "It's the god who brought the orb."

While they watched with amazement and wonder, the orb split like an egg, and the top hemisphere hovered above the bottom before slowly gliding open on an un-seen hinge in the back. Resting in the center of the orb were three small globes, similar to the spherical gems that studded the outer surface, pulsating with the same veins of inner golden fire...only these seemed to have a living light inside them, something amorphous and swirling. The tones appeared to be arising from their vibration. The birds twittering in the canopy fell into sync with it and attuned their avian voices to the music of the Treasure Star, until the music of the jungle was the music of the spheres, and the whole canopy was alive with one song.

Nebula's breath came in excited huffs. "Simeon...what on Earth is this?"

Croom gazed upon the relic with equal fascination. "It's...I don't know. I've never seen anything like it."

Chief Towhiit reached in a curious finger as the glow-ing globes throbbed and sang. As soon as his skin made contact, the golden orb erupted in a blinding flash that made everyone present clench their eyes shut tightly and turn their faces for fear of having their vision seared away. The chief was no exception. He dropped the golden orb and covered his eyes as the two halves of the relic shut together with a thunderous *boom* that shook the Zingaloo village and rattled their bones. The Treasure Star landed on the ground with a resounding *thunk* and sank further into the packed soil than an object with so little weight should have been physically able to.

The strange tones fell silent, and the jungle became calm once again.

No one made a sound, until Croom broke the fascinat-ed silence as only he could. "Well...I don't think anyone saw *that* coming."

Chief Towhiit blinked until his vision returned. Then he crouched low and picked up the orb to find that a second jeweled sphere had broken free of its setting, leaving two empty ringed divots in the golden surface now. The opening had been fused shut, and the strange shape was now melted and amorphous, as if all the sharp edges of it had been softened under great heat. The chief rubbed the orb, and he pressed on it with the tips of his broad fingers, and squeezed the orb with both of his powerful hands as if he was trying to crush a melon to reach the seeds inside. It didn't so much as wobble under his great strength.

Nebula shook off the dazzle that had stunned her senses. "I don't know what to make...of any of this."

Croom had little idea, either. But that had never stopped him from waxing philosophic about anything, and it wouldn't stop him from doing that very thing in this instance, either. "It simply proves that there are forces beyond our understanding at work in the world, Neb. Perhaps there really were gods in the stars for the ancient Zingaloo. Perhaps what Thoiink was trying to return truly belonged to them." He eyed the orb and all of its mystifying magic. "Perhaps we stand now in the presence of tribal divinity."

Nebula was far too pragmatic to let any of that be the truth. She wasn't certain how any of what she'd just witnessed could be even remotely possible. But she also saw the joyous wonder and collective fascination in the Zingaloo tribe as they passed the relic from hand to eager hand, turning it and gazing at it as if their belief in the old gods had just undergone an unexpected resurgence. She had no other choice than to set aside her logic for the moment, if only to keep her head from hurting at the thought of it all.

The chief approached Croom with the loose jewel sphere in his palm. He held it out happily, smiled, and nodded with excited eyes. "*Clopclop-click*?" he asked.

"Oh yes, Chief," Croom agreed. "It certainly *is* spectacular."

Chief Towhiit smiled wider and nodded more emphatically. "*Cliiiick-pop-poppop-doink!*" He pushed the globe into Croom's hand and folded his fingers down around it.

Croom's face became grave and stony. "Oh, we couldn't possibly take this as a thank you gift," Croom said, first in English, then in Zingali. "This little beauty belongs to the Treasure Star, and the Treasure Star belongs to the Zingaloo; it might be crucial to the orb in a way we wouldn't fully understand. I feel guilty enough having broken off the one I gave Horatio."

After seeing the great significance the orb held for the tribe, Nebula easily agreed with Croom's assessment that it should remain with them. "He's right," she told the chief, though he couldn't understand a word she said. "This is yours, as much as the rest is."

"*Clickpop-click-click-click-doink-fwiiiiip-thip-thip*," Chief Towhiit replied. The tribesmen raised their spears in Croom and Nebula's direction in a most menacing fashion, and an instantaneous change of spirit, from joyous exultation to forced generosity.

Croom cringed. "Oh. Well...okay, then." He took the sphere from the chief and rolled it in his hand, admiring again the weight and solidity and strange properties of a mineral he'd never seen before. "Very kind of you."

The Zingaloo lowered their spears, and all of their smiles returned simultaneously.

"What did he say that changed your mind?" Nebula whispered through her nose in that charming yet slightly disturbing way she had.

"He told me that the gems on the outside appear to be nothing more than decoration, so what would be the harm in us taking one."

"Still, it doesn't seem right," Nebula insisted.

"He also said that the last person to refuse his generosity was fed to alligators until there was nothing left of him but toenails and eyelashes."

Nebula blinked. "I suppose we *could* take it home with us after all."

Croom grinned and scratched his ear. "If they insist."

TEN

"And that, my friends, is how the Jeweled Sphere of the Zingaloo came to reside in the Vanished Civilizations, Mythical Creatures, and Artifacts of Incredible Antiquity wing of Hydewhite Museum."

Simeon Croom was back to his dapper self, with his bow tie spiffy and angular, his collar sleekly ironed, and his glasses round and shiny and reflecting the happy, hopeful faces of a new crush of museum goers eager to learn about the camouflaged tribe hidden in the heart of the Sarabezi jungle. Between his lectern and the crowd was a glass cube larger than a breadbox but smaller than a single-bedroom apartment in Haven City, with a gilded goblet that nested the blue-opal sphere from the orb in its pristine cup. It looked like a glob of sky filled with lightning; its golden veins shimmered like a desert mirage and cast sparkles on the walls like a rain of blue light all around the chamber. For being second prize in the quest for the Treasure Star of the Zingaloo, it was none too shabby.

"Thank you for that scintillating introduction to a most fascinating culture, Mr. Croom—your stories never cease to entertain!" said the docent, starstruck by his crooked grin as she led the group out of the hall and toward the next exhibit.

Croom leaned on his lectern, staring into the glass case and hungrily eating up the artifact with both eyes.

"It's quite a tasty morsel, isn't it?" Nebula Everhope said as she quietly entered the room.

"Thoroughly delicious," Croom sighed.

"And yet, we know nothing of the substance it's made of, or its true origin."

"Perhaps we'll learn all of that one day," Croom told her. "For now, we should simply allow the mystery and behold the wonder."

"And what about the idea of Shtaaa?" she asked, knowing her credulous nature had little room for such strangeness, in spite of everything she'd seen.

Croom's forehead slumped. "What about it?"

"The relic from the myth exists, which means it had to come from somewhere. And the song it sang, and the swirling light...the way it captivated everyone who witnessed it. It was...otherworldly."

Croom smiled. "I couldn't have chosen a better word, Neb."

"So do you truly believe it's possible that ancient gods gave the orb to the Zingaloo, and that it can bestow immortality to those who live in its presence?"

Croom wasn't prepared to say he didn't believe...but he wasn't ready to say that he did believe, either. "The fantasy mixed with the reality of it all makes for a heady cocktail, doesn't it, Neb? Something to keep our imaginations percolating and our minds wide open to *all* the possibilities."

"I suppose it does," Nebula replied. "The board seems thoroughly satisfied with your results, at least...even Roderick Fulk."

It wasn't at all surprising to Croom. "Isn't it funny how recovered treasure and an increase in paid attendance to the museum can soften even the hardest of bureaucratic hearts?"

Nebula couldn't help but notice a twinge of remorse in his voice. "Then why don't you sound entirely satisfied with your accomplishments?"

Croom thought back to the exhilaration he felt during the his ride in a stone rocket launched from the throat of a volcano, and the incredible calm he felt when parachuting from the peak to the base when he'd finally found the Treasure Star; the wind had tousled his hair mercilessly like a loving grandfather saying "Welcome home, kiddo!" and he had a previously undiscovered ancient treasure hidden in his knapsack. And that was to say nothing of the sheer amazement he'd felt when the chief opened the orb and released all that music, all that brilliance! One anthropological mystery of the ancients had been solved thanks to his intrepid spirit and his refusal to turn around and go back to the museum empty-handed...and yet several others had now been revealed, to be wondered about and explored. It was beyond thrilling, even simply to recall it now. There would never be a feeling to replace that, and he knew it. "Because satisfaction is the death-knell of discovery," he said finally. "And I know now what it means to surrender to it."

Nebula paused to let him have his moment.

She thought five dramatic, wistful sighs from him was "moment" plenty.

"I know he's not a savory character in your personal mythology anymore," she said as kindly as possible, "but tell me honestly now that the Treasure Star appears to be far more significant than just an historical relic from a culture presumed long-extinct: why do you think Dr. Bombfell *really* wanted you to find it for him? Do you genuinely believe it was so he could be paid for services rendered?"

Croom shook his head slowly, deliberately, as if he'd already asked himself the same question but had failed to arrive at a proper answer. "Horatio's grandparents died in a shipwreck after he graduated from Mount Tumbledown and left him a considerable sum. He's been independently wealthy for years...he doesn't need to be paid for anything."

Nebula felt a tingle at the base of her skull. "Unless he wasn't expecting to be paid monetarily..."

"Yes...it certainly seems he's fallen elbow-deep in something dark and significant." Though he'd known the whole time that some sort of duplicity was likely to be at play, he still sounded crestfallen as he said it aloud, as if the true implications of his compromised friendship with Bombfell were only now sinking in.

Nebula tsked. "It sounds more like he climbed down into it willingly."

"Ha!" Croom barked at her comment. "Your clarity never fails to entertain!"

"And what do you think he'll do when he realizes the stone you gave him wasn't the actual Treasure Star?" Nebula asked, not mincing words. "The press coverage for the Jeweled Sphere is going to draw his attention for certain. He'll know you don't have it either."

"I suppose he'll circle back around to my doorstep at some point," Croom said as he walked to the glass case and polished a fingerprint off of it with his cuff, "to either exact his vengeance, or to beg my forgiveness and try to explain away his atrocious behavior and devious dealings. Perhaps both, even."

"And what if he returns to the Sarabezi in a rage to take the Treasure Star by force from the Zingaloo?" Her words rang with a severe and indignant truth.

The thought had crossed Croom's mind more than a few times on their journey back to Haven City, and even more than that after they'd settled back at Hydewhite. "Their tribe has persevered for two thousand years through an expertise in hiding and an indomitable capability to survive in a largely hostile environment. And while we may never have seen them launch those spears, they made clearly known that they are fierce defenders of their own best interests. Surely Horatio Bombfell would pose no threat they couldn't handily take care of."

"But the shadowy agency he works for just might."

Croom had considered that as well. "I'm sure they'll be fine."

"Your friend gone rogue turned into an adversary who pointed a gun at you—and *me*, as a matter of fact—and stole what he thought was a relic that actually isn't, and you're sure the Zingaloo will be fine if he chooses to retaliate?"

Croom frowned. "Your penny seems to have no shiny side, Nebula Everhope," he told her. "You should work on that."

Nebula took slight offense at this, which was a fine return to form. "And you should work on figuring out who to trust and when to trust them," she snapped. "Perhaps you could avoid running off at a moment's notice to find an artifact halfway around the world with someone who was only using your superior skills because he had none of his own to offer the cause."

"Did we not have an adventure, Neb?" Croom asked her in reply. "Did we not discover a culture no one had even seen in several lifetimes, and return their sacred relic to them, and wing our way home with an equal treasure in our possession that renewed the museum's faith in us?"

Nebula wouldn't allow it. "And did we even know who we were in league with while all of this was happening thousands of miles away in a land whose language we couldn't understand?"

"Well, some of us could..." Croom smirked.

"That is entirely beside the point, Simeon!"

He shrugged. "You're the one who brought it up."

A clatter of footsteps echoed through the room as the pair watched a shadow emerge from the entryway. "Pardon me for intruding on your argument—very rude of me, I know."

"You're in a public museum, sir," Croom replied. "There's no such thing as an intrusion in one of those! It is we who should apologize for the awkward exchange."

"*You* should apologize," Nebula pushed.

"I just said that," Croom retorted.

"No apologies necessary, really," said the older gentleman as he stepped forward and removed his coal-gray fedora. "A young woman named Gilda pointed me in this direction...I was told I could find Simeon Croom here."

"And so you have," Nebula confirmed.

"Goodness," the man said. "You're much more presentable in person than you appear in your newspaper photographs, Mr. Croom. So dashing and cinematic!"

"Why, thank you for that—I like your hat and your manners!" Croom offered back. "And who are you, exactly?"

"My name is Henderson Manning...however, the people who know me best call me Dinsworth. It's something of a family joke, you see."

Croom didn't catch the comedy, if indeed there was any to be caught. "No...I don't see at all."

"That's part of the joke!"

Nebula laughed, not because she recognized the humor, but because she found it rewarding to make Croom feel as if he wasn't quite in on the fun.

"And what is it that I can do for you, sir?" Croom asked.

"Well, I've applied for the assistant position listed in the Haven City Gazette last week."

Neither Croom nor Nebula recalled placing an advertisement before they left for the Sarabezi. "Are you certain it was Civilizations, Creatures, and Antiquities that the job was listed for?"

Dinsworth's eyes sparkled. "Oh yes...I wouldn't have applied for it otherwise."

It was unexpected, but there was always room for more help. "Well," Croom said, "I suppose we could conduct an interview to see if—"

"Your board members interviewed me this morning," Dinsworth informed him cheerfully as he fidgeted with the brim of his hat. "Two gentlemen by the names of Roderick Fulk and Martin Ayers."

"They did?" Nebula asked.

"Oh, yes—wonderful chaps, both!"

Croom marveled at how presumptuous a move this was on the part of the board—a power play to remind him of his place in the pecking order, no doubt. "Then I suppose we could figure out something for you to—"

"They informed me that I should report to you directly to learn what responsibilities will be involved with your travels."

"My travels?" Croom encountered very few situations he couldn't babble his way through. But the board had hired an assistant for him without notifying him first, and the position pertained to his travels, of which he had no knowledge.

This situation was a non-babbler, for certain.

"They told me you'd be heading out on walkabouts quite frequently from here forward," Dinsworth explained, "that there was such demand for new artifacts for this wing that your travel schedule was certain to keep you busy for the foreseeable future."

"Hmmm..." Croom said, scratching his chin in that charming, thoughtful manner he had. "It sounds as if the museum has just answered the questions regarding my future."

"How lovely it would have been if they'd thought to clue us in so we could prepare for it ourselves," Nebula commented. "We'll find something that can benefit from your attention, Dinsworth, though we have no idea what your qualifications might be."

"Terribly sorry for the confusion of all this," Dinsworth said. "Perhaps I should debrief you about myself, my dear?"

Unlike when Bombfell said it, Nebula didn't mind this version of that endearment; it didn't make her feel like she might need to bathe in a lake of fire in order to rinse the verbal filth away from her skin. Dinsworth's version was comforting instead, almost like hearing the words come from her father. In fact, it wasn't the only fatherly aspect she recognized in him, which made her feel instantly at ease with their new associate.

"Over tea and small sandwiches?" she suggested.

"Delightful!" Dinsworth crooned as they walked toward the exit.

"Are you coming, Simeon?" Nebula called back over her shoulder. "Or should we just leave you here gazing into space for the custodians to dust like the other relics?" Dinsworth laughed at her joke, and she knew in an instant she would love having him around.

Croom's imagination was already wandering through all the possibilities of what his next adventure might be. "I do believe it's time to revisit the Journal of Journeys and see where I left off," he said, entirely ignoring her question.

Dinsworth's eyes lit with excitement, while Nebula's rolled skyward. "You'll get used to this sort of thing," she said.

"Is it something *you've* gotten used to?" Dinsworth asked.

Nebula grimaced. "Not in the least."

Dinsworth laughed. "Oh, Mr. Croom? I nearly forgot! Gilda asked me to bring you this as well." He handed Croom a letter with no return address, and no postage stamp or cancellation in the corner to tell him where it had arrived from.

"Fan mail, I would assume," Croom said with an irritating wink. "It's probably going to be pouring in from here on out."

Nebula refused to be impressed by what was more likely to be an electric bill or a notification of overdue library books. She simply tugged on Dinsworth's arm and guided him toward the office. "Now...tell me what you know about vanished cultures and items of great antiquity."

"Well, I inherited an antique pocket watch from my great-uncle several years ago, but his culture had vanished long before then..."

Their voices disappeared as Croom slid his finger beneath the flap of the envelope and removed the letter, which was a piece of translucent paper folded crisply in equal thirds. When he flipped it open, he found that it wasn't an actual letter at all, but rather a challenge; a gauntlet thrown down via post by a most familiar figure, coming as a largely-expected next move in a contest Croom hadn't even realized had begun until he saw it. The paper held only a watermark of an all-too-familiar image: a black circle interrupted by a falling bomb, with finely-scripted words written underneath that read simply:

Our final adventure has only begun, my friend.

An unsettling tingle shimmered up Simeon Croom's spine as if he'd been touched by electricity. He scratched his chin and wondered aloud, "What on Earth have you gotten us into this time, Horatio?"

EPILOGUE

The blue-opal orb with its flashing gold veins may have been otherworldly and overwhelmingly lovely to look at, but it was useless in the greater scheme of things to those who sought the real relic. "We sent you into the Sarabezi to retrieve the Treasure Star, and you returned with a paperweight." It dropped onto the mahogany desk with a *thunk* that sounded out like a small thunderclap in the cavernous study. "You're an idiot."

"Yes, I realize now that it isn't what we were expecting, though it was much more difficult to discern while it was happening." Perhaps for the first time in his arrogant, accomplished life, Horatio Bombfell actually sounded repentant. "No one is more chagrinned at my failure than I."

"Your theatrics won't be tolerated by Ex M, Dr. Bombfell. You cloud the waters when you behave like this, and that will prevent us from achieving our objective. I was certain I'd made that clear to you when you agreed to be a part of this organization."

"Yes, but I had assumed—"

He wasn't allowed to finish. "Silver Six are working under strict guidelines which cannot afford to be compromised by your careless assumptions. Neither you nor Croom has the Treasure Star in your possession, which was the entire purpose of your endeavor, was it not?"

Bombfell cringed at the wretched sensation of his superiority rising up at such an inopportune moment, knowing he wasn't free to express it in the least. "I...don't know how it went so wrong."

"It only matters that it never goes *so wrong* again."

Bombfell agreed with a nervous twitch of his head. "What can I do to make things right?"

The dark figure issuing the veiled threats stood from an oversized leather chair, its hinges creaking a diabolical chorus of praise as he rose. "You'll return to the Sarabezi, of course, and retrieve the real Treasure Star from the Zingaloo post-haste, by whatever means are necessary. Am I understood?"

Bombfell sneered. "I'll do whatever it takes to fetch the artifact."

"Good. And then you'll make certain the other relics on our list are recovered without similar magnanimous displays by Mr. Croom. We simply cannot proceed without them. You know as well as I what will happen should there be any further failure." A square cufflink of clean silver gleamed in a stray beam that streamed through the window, revealing the strange impression of a symbol on its surface that looked very much like a square star overlaid by a hollow ring, with an arrowhead ray emanating from its base. A moment later, a swarm of ravenous gray clouds swallowed the sun whole, and the gleam was gone.

Bombfell pushed down a lump in his throat, made of equal parts terror and unfettered excitement. "I certainly do."

Without further comment, he turned and left the study, his heart thundering and his mind crackling with plans for what was coming, and what his reward would be for helping bring it about.

To be continued...

THANK YOU SO MUCH FOR READING SIMEON CROOM AND THE TREASURE STAR!

Indie authors live and die by their review profiles, so if you liked what you read, or even if you didn't, please consider clicking over to Amazon.com and leaving an honest review. As Croom would say, "It's a smashing good thing you do for the sake of the literary world, friend!" Steven agrees wholeheartedly with that assessment.

SIMEON CROOM
AND THE HAND OF FATIQ

THE CHRONICLES OF CROOM BOOK 2

Simeon Croom is back to his adventuresome ways and headed into the Mukarrah Desert to decrypt mysterious riddle-glyphs found in the newly discovered underground pyramid-tomb of an ancient Kharamian boy prince! This time, our dashing hero is in search of the Hand of Fatiq, a gauntlet that offers the wearer supernatural protection from all enemies. But Croom isn't the only one with an interest in the relic, and the others conspiring to make the discovery will stop at nothing to claim their prize...

The Hand of Fatiq, the second book in the Chronicles of Croom, will take Simeon and friends deeper into the growing mystery of Silver Six and Ex M as they delve beneath the desert sands seeking answers, pursuing ancient treasures, and uncovering even more questions as they go...for history, antiquity, renown!

COMING SOON!

Steven Luna almost never knows what to do with his hands in social situations. He's a continual embarrassment to the human genome, but it seems to make people laugh, so he's chosen to just go with it. He's the author of the absurdly humorous Joe Vampire series for grown-ups, the heart-wrenchingly serious Songs from the Phenomenal Nothing for almost-grown-ups, and a bunch of other stories all over the internet, suitable for anyone who can find them.

Find him online:

www.twitter.com/thestevenluna
www.facebook.com/thestevenluna
www.thestevenluna.wordpress.com

ACKNOWLEDGEMENTS

Great love and endless thanks to my wife Marie, as always; I'm no Simeon Croom, to be certain, but she is unmistakably the order-keeping Nebula Everhope in my world, the cosmos to my chaos, and I would fall off the mountain without her. Love as well to my kids, who are treasures beyond treasure, wonders beyond wonder, and proof enough for me that the universe is indeed full of magic, and that it somehow saw fit to send an incredible lot of it my way. Soaring gratitude to my family and friends who support my creative bent, even when it somehow leads away from a logical path...in other words: every single time. A tip o' the fedora in thanks to the Gents, Benjamin Wallace and Jordon Quattlebaum, for their tremendous inspiration, grand encouragement, and rousing "onward-ho!" spirit as Croom came to his conclusion at Dapper Summit 2016 (and at all other times as well, of course). And every gratitude in the wide, round world to Clayton Smith, a champion above champions, an amazing partner through the adventuresome wilderness of storytelling and bookcraft, and a thoroughly extraordinary friend in all else. This story may have started out to be something in particular when I wrote it, but it ended up as something far stronger when he edited it (twice, even), and I can't possibly thank him enough for everything.

Find these other wonderful titles from

at www.dapperpress.com/library and Amazon!

By Clayton Smith

Apocalypticon

Three years have passed since the Jamaicans caused the apocalypse, and things in post-Armageddon Chicago have settled into a new kind of normal. Unfortunately, that "normal" includes collapsing skyscrapers, bands of bloodthirsty maniacs, and a dwindling cache of survival supplies. After watching his family, friends, and most of the non-sadistic elements of society crumble around him, Patrick decides it's time to cross one last item off his bucket list: he's going to Disney World.

Anomaly Flats

Somewhere just off the interstate, in the heart of the American Midwest, there's a quaint, quirky town where the stars in the sky circle a hypnotic void....where magnetic fields play havoc with time and perception...where metallic rain and plasma rivers and tentacles in the plumbing are simply part of the unsettling charm. Mallory Jenkins is about to experience the unique properties of this place for herself...

It Came From Anomaly Flats

The oddest little town in the Midwest has a thousand demented stories to tell...some of them are horrifying enough to send shivers down the strongest of spines. In this first collected volume of chill-inducing stories from everyone's favorite transdimensional town, you'll find reason enough to question your own sanity, even as you try to reassure yourself that things like this only happen in stories. Don't they? Welcome to Anomaly Flats. How loud can you scream?

Mabel Gray and the Wizard who Swallowed the Sun

All is not well in Brightsbane, the village of eternal night. An evil wizard—the very wizard who swallowed the sun, in fact—has stolen The Boneyard Compendium, a book of powerful spells that could bring about the destruction of the entire town. Mabel Gray sets out to find the three keys of bone that unlock the Compendium before the wizard gets his diabolical hands on them.

Na Akua

Maui was supposed to be a romantic trip for two. But when Grayson Park's bride leaves him at the altar, a solo trip to paradise seems like just the thing to take him far from his troubles. Then he meets the beautiful and enigmatic Hi'iaka, and his troubles just begin—because when she's abducted by the sinister Kamapua'a, a savage creature bent on draining her life by the light of the full moon, she calls on Grayson to rescue her. With his loyal, new-found Hawaiian friend Polunu as his steadfast guide, Grayson sets out on an incredible adventure that pits him against the very gods of Hawaiian mythology.

Pants on Fire

A circus performer leaving behind a trail of ghosts; a castle of bumbling nitwits desperate to prove themselves to King Arthur; a world full of deadly mirrors; a librarian who mistakes Death for a very somber wheat farmer; this pesky little thing called "the Rapture." All these and more pepper the pages of Pants on Fire: A Collection of Lies, a twisted, quirky, macabre world full of hilarious and chilling tales. Being lied to has never been so much fun!

By Clayton Smith and Percy Rodriguez

Death and McCootie

A film noir-style, madcap farce that goes a little haywire when the Grim Reaper tries to collect the soul of Edgar P. McCootie, a hapless private investigator in 1940s Chicago. Chaos ensues when McCootie hits on Death's weakness for a long-shot gamble and switches places with the Grim Reaper in a bet to save his soul.

By Jordon Quattlebaum

Breakdown (Episodes 1 – 8)

When Thomas Monroe's car breaks down on the side of the road, he's sure the day can't get any worse... until he receives a mysterious call warning him of impending doom. Seconds later, the United States is his by what appears to be an electromagnetic pulse, knocking the power grid almost completely offline. Thom, like most of the country, is unprepared. Worst of all, his daughter, the only family he has left, is halfway across the state at college... and the world between them is a warzone.

Running on Empty: Preacher and Ghost, Issue #1

Nearly 80 years have passed since a meteor struck the Earth, sending plumes of dust into the atmosphere to create the Great Eclipse. Generations of survivors have grown up without the sun, their days barely brighter than their long, cold nights. Information travels from Citadel to Citadel, changing with each retelling, like a childhood game of telephone. Archivists toil to piece together fragments of truth from the myriad of rumors that blow into town, selling the truth to the trade guilds for a profit.